Ethan Roam suffers from night terrors and vivid daydreams, which lead him to the doorstep of the eccentric Dr. Grady Hunter, who thrusts him into a world of supernatural misfits. Ethan quickly learns that there's more reality to his dreams than he suspected.

As Ethan unravels the truth behind his nightmares and falls into his first experience with love, he also finds himself the target of a sinister plan.

Ethan's trust in his new companions will be tested and he'll have to decide who he can rely on and who he must defy in order to survive a fatal Halloween night.

ROAM

Roam, Book One

Dez Schwartz

A NineStar Press Publication

Published by NineStar Press
P.O. Box 91792,
Albuquerque, New Mexico, 87199 USA.
www.ninestarpress.com

Roam

Printed in the USA
First Edition
October, 2018

Print ISBN: 978-1-949340-89-1

Also available in eBook, ISBN: 978-1-949340-83-9

Special thanks to my loving family for all of their support
and encouragement.

I dedicate this book to all the dreamers.

One: Daydreams

"HE'S HERE," A voice whispered. Ethan Roam struggled to assess his surroundings, but his vision was blurry. All he could make out were a few trees around him. Only one thing was clear before him. The girl.

She was the same girl he had seen many times before in his dreams. She was slender and meek with fiery red hair and kind blue eyes. Subtle freckles accented her nose and her lips were the color of cherry blossoms. She wore strange clothes. Each time, they were different, which Ethan wondered if that was normal for a recurring dream. They were crafted from organic materials he couldn't quite pinpoint.

"Hello?" she urged, as though trying to wake him; although, he wondered why since he was staring right at her. Her expression was dire, as though she was speaking *at* him instead of *to* him. She pursed her lips with a hint of anxiety and then tried again. "Hello? You have to hurry. He's here!"

Ethan's heart pounded. He wanted to greet her or ask who she was talking about. This was his fifth time to have the same dream. Each time, she tried to talk to him, and he could never say anything in response. He sluggishly tried to get the words to flow past his lips. He strained forward to be closer to her, and for a split second, her eyes widened as if she'd finally seen a reaction from him.

To his left, twigs snapped and a deep growl rumbled. He turned in time to see a massive wolf tearing toward them.

He screamed as he moved to block the girl from the wolf, and then everything faded away...

Ethan sat up with a start, realizing he'd fallen asleep during Dr. Wallace's history class. The professor, annoyed at having been interrupted during one of his favorite lectures, balled his hands into fists and placed them firmly on his hips as he stared disapprovingly at Ethan. The rest of the class was quick to stare, too, only they were less annoyed and more amused, much to Ethan's embarrassment.

"SO, YEAH... PRETTY sure I'm going to switch classes now. I can't imagine going back there." Ethan had finished recounting his literal and figurative nightmare to his good friend, Dr. Arthur Ellis.

Arthur let out a jolly laugh at the idea of Ethan screaming during Dr. Wallace's lecture.

"I wish I could've seen the look on the old bulldog's face." He grinned, wiping a humored tear from his eye.

"Trust me, you don't. I'm pretty sure he was imagining my gruesome demise since he was all hyped on Greek war talk. Nope, never going back there again."

Arthur was an old friend of Ethan's mother, Karen, and Ethan had known him for most of his life. Arthur, a portly and generally jovial man, was around so much Ethan thought of him like an unofficial uncle of sorts. Being a professor seemed to fit him perfectly as he had a studious look to him and felt the need to educate others on all matters he deemed himself an expert at, which was nearly everything. Ethan found his positivity both admirable and enviable. Talking to Arthur always seemed to help calm his nerves and so he found himself opening up to him constantly when he usually blocked the rest of the world out.

Recovering from the humor of the situation, Arthur scratched his graying beard as if asking it if he should pry. The beard seemed to concur, so he peered over his glasses and across his desk to where Ethan sat.

"Are your dreams becoming more frequent?"

Ethan sat up a little straighter as the tone of the conversation shifted. He glanced nervously at a dream catcher that was hanging near a bookcase cluttered with old tomes and artifacts. A feather appeared to flutter but then lay perfectly still against the wall.

Although an English professor, Dr. Arthur Ellis specialized in folklore. It was his favorite topic in the world and would talk about it at length, given the opportunity. His office was decorated appropriately. That is to say, he'd immersed himself in items his guests would find interesting, thus giving himself the opportunity to engage in discourse on the subject. And if his guests did not ask questions, then he would gladly inform them about the carefully curated decor anyway.

"Define *more frequent*," Ethan answered coyly but then sighed and opened up. "You know I've always had dreams like that. Where I'm in strange places and being attacked by weird creatures. Nightmares, really."

"The only dreams you ever have," Arthur concurred.

Ethan tried to explain. For years, the girl with the fiery red hair had appeared in his dreams and nightmares as what he believed to be a symbol for something, but now that she was talking to him...it was kind of creeping him out. "You know the girl isn't new. And...she's interacting more with me now. She's not just there, you know? She's a character in my dream rather than a figure in the background." Ethan tried to explain.

"And what about the wolf?"

"It was the same one." Ethan stared into his palms as he tried to recall details. "Large, black fur, saliva dripping from his mouth...but when he ran at me, he ran standing up." He frowned as he remembered the disgusting appearance of the creature.

Arthur cut in with enthusiasm. "Like a werewolf!"

"I guess..." Ethan considered the details more closely, but the more he thought about it, the harder it was for them to remain clear. "I'm not really sure. But here's the thing, I'm dreaming during the day now. These all used to happen at night. Today during class wasn't the first time it's happened; just the first time anyone witnessed it. And I wasn't even entirely asleep."

Arthur seemed to listen with great interest, and when the last sentence rolled from Ethan's lips, he leaned forward with a graceful and what appeared to be genuine curiosity only a well learned academic could pull off.

Ethan continued, "I remember everything Doctor Wallace was saying. It was like I was in two places at once. The dream overlapped onto reality until I woke up... screaming, apparently."

Arthur provided the same considerate but serious suggestion he'd already offered a few times before. "Have you considered talking to anyone about this?"

"I'm talking to someone now," Ethan quipped, but he knew what Arthur really meant. He'd been nudging Ethan to go to a doctor for years, but Ethan hated doctors. Especially, he hated the idea he might have some weird medical condition that would require him to *go* to a doctor.

"Someone more qualified than myself." Arthur smiled patiently.

"Hey, you are *Doctor* Ellis."

Arthur seemed to criticize him over his glasses with an impatient stare.

"I don't like people," Ethan retorted stubbornly, knowing he was losing the argument.

"Who does?" He pulled a card out of his wallet and handed it to Ethan.

"I've been holding on to this for a while. Until I felt the time was right," he explained as Ethan read the business card. "He's an old friend of mine. I really think you should go and talk to him. I have reason to believe he might have a *unique* perspective on these dreams of yours."

Maybe Arthur was right. If his sleep problems were finally getting in the way of his daily activities, then maybe it was time to be proactive about them.

"Aren't all your friends, like your collectibles, unique?" Ethan teased, as he slipped the card into his pocket.

"You know me." Arthur nodded, relaxing into his chair now he'd won their battle of wills. "I love a good backstory. Oh, and don't tell your mother," Arthur added. "She hates it when I meddle."

Ethan smiled and rolled his eyes as he left the office. "We all do."

Two: The Interview

ETHAN TOOK A deep calming breath and then entered the building through its glass doors. He tried to appear confident by standing straight and readjusted the strap on his messenger bag so it wasn't slouching off his shoulder.

The general interior design of the office was black and silver with the occasional splash of deep purple. On a glass coffee table in front of a few black leather chairs, where magazines were normally spread out, was a peculiar book that proclaimed itself an almanac and a deck of tarot cards. Ethan eyed them suspiciously as they weren't something one would expect to see lying around a doctor's office.

All Kinds Welcome
Dr. Grady Hunter
222S. Onyx Ave.

Ethan read the business card again to make sure he was at the right place. He hadn't been able to schedule an appointment since the card provided no number, so he'd decided to go in person and ask.

Directly in front of him was the receptionist's desk and it was similarly decorated with a scrying ball on one side and what appeared to be a Ouija board directly across from it. It was hard to tell because there were books and file folders stacked on top. It was as if he'd accidentally stepped into a fortune-teller's shop instead of a medical office.

Sitting behind the desk was a young, waifish woman with pale skin and short black hair bobbed to frame her jawline. Her bangs were cut perfectly straight, which created a bold effect around her already angular face. She wore a simple sleeveless black dress Ethan thought was questionably low cut for a professional office.

The woman lifted her attention from her computer and gave him the once-over with her piercing blue eyes, which unsettled him.

Hanging loosely from her neck and accenting the deep cut of her dress was an art deco–inspired necklace with a silver chain holding a charm designed to be a bird of some sort. Ethan guessed it was supposed to be a swan emerging from a flower or some similar allegory.

"Can I help you?" she asked with a crisp tone to divert his eyes away from her neckline. Her bright pink lipstick and overly rouged cheeks were a stark contrast to the rest of her appearance. She took out an appointment ledger and scanned it, presumably to see whom he might be. He couldn't help but notice that she'd matched her nail polish to the pop of color in her makeup.

"M-my name is Ethan Roam. I didn't make an appointment. S-sorry. I was hoping to walk in." He stuttered in spite of his efforts to not seem nervous.

Vivian Edwards, according to the nameplate on her desk, waved him toward one of the chairs and stated simply, "Doctor Hunter will be out in a minute. You may wait there. Make yourself comfortable." She resumed typing and ignoring his existence.

The cold greeting from the woman had only made him more uncomfortable. Ethan moved to the chair as instructed, but before he was seated, another figure entered the room.

The young man, dressed in Rocket Dog sneakers, jeans, and a carelessly unbuttoned blue plaid shirt with a black Scooby Doo T-shirt underneath, was quite the opposite of Vivian. He had a perk to his step, a smile on his face, and a sparkle to his brown eyes. He was humming a tune that sounded suspiciously like a Three Dog Night song as he entered the room. His appearance brought a pleasantness to the space that hadn't been there before as he strutted in and grabbed the folders on Vivian's desk.

The man, who seemed to be around the same age as Ethan, finally noticed his presence and stopped humming. He grinned and glanced at Vivian, nodding in Ethan's direction. "Who's the new guy?"

Vivian didn't stop typing but answered shortly, "He's here to be interviewed."

Interviewed? Oh...the doctor will probably want to find out what my symptoms are before he takes me on as a patient, Ethan reasoned to himself as he sat awkwardly, shifting positions in his chair.

"Oh! Can't wait." The man turned on his heel and exited to his hidden office around the corner, peeking over his shoulder at Ethan before he disappeared.

Vivian rolled her eyes. "That's Benny. He's an idiot."

"He seemed...nice," Ethan responded, trying to be polite.

Vivian gave him another once-over with her piercing gaze, and then she settled into her work again without another word.

"Not a great bedside manner, but I like her brazen honesty. Although, I find the word *naïve* suits him best. He's not actually an idiot," a deep but charming voice chimed in.

"Debatable," Vivian murmured.

The voice had a British lilt to it that was clearly beginning to fall away with American influence. Ethan turned to discover a tall man with blond wavy hair that was brushed to one side. He appeared in his mid-thirties, which was surprising since Ethan had been expecting someone more around Arthur's age.

Dr. Grady Hunter was a stunning figure, dressed in charcoal-gray slacks and a matching unbuttoned sports coat. The ensemble was paired with a gray pressed button-up shirt underneath. He'd missed fastening a couple of buttons, and it hung open a bit loosely at the top. Despite his tall and slim frame he had broad shoulders and high cheekbones, which made him classically handsome and slightly intimidating. Ethan would have felt diminutive next to him if it weren't for the man's charismatic smile and kind gray eyes that made him seem friendly and down to earth.

Grady greeted him with a nod and opened his office door wide. "Welcome, Ethan. Please, come in."

Grady indicated for Ethan to take a seat, and then he rounded his desk and also sat, carefully studying Ethan's every move.

"Sorry for not making an appointment, Doctor Hunter," Ethan said, unsure of how to start things off.

"No need for apologies. And I insist you call me Grady." The doctor smiled pleasantly. "Arthur advised you might be stopping by."

"Oh," Ethan acknowledged, a little annoyed at his friend's presumptuous behavior. "That's good."

"Indeed." Grady grabbed a pen and a form from his top desk drawer as Ethan watched anxiously.

"Ethan Roam," stated Grady, writing his name on the top of the form. "Let's get to it, shall we?"

Ethan motioned that he was ready, although he was very distracted. He'd imagined the office would be more sterile, like most doctors' offices, but instead, he found himself in a room that was more of a private study. There was even a fireplace, though he noted it was a faux one.

Grady jumped right to it. "What are your qualifications?"

Qualifications. Ethan attempted to focus. *I guess he means why I'm here.*

"Well, I've been having night terrors for a few years now. I dream vicious creatures are attacking me in my sleep, and I wake feeling like I'm still in the nightmare. My body is paralyzed sometimes, so I'm aware I'm awake, but I can't move, which causes me to panic. Recently, though, it's gotten worse because now I'm also dreaming during the day."

"Is that it?"

Ethan shrugged. "Pretty much."

"Damn. I thought it'd be something more interesting," Grady muttered in disappointment.

Ethan, taken aback by the doctor's reaction, was offended.

"W-well. They're pretty awful. I was attacked by a werewolf yesterday."

Grady's eyebrows flew upward, and his eyes became intense and inquisitive. "Really? Where?"

"In the dream. The daydream." Ethan wondered if Arthur had sent him here as part of a bad practical joke.

"Ah..." Grady's energetic demeanor subsided, and he quickly returned to his former casual self.

"All right, then. Do you have any past experience?"

"No, that's it really," Ethan answered limply.

Grady set down his pen and form. He leaned back in his chair, eying Ethan considerately. "All right. These next few questions are standard procedure. Please answer them honestly."

Ethan nodded that he understood.

"Do you believe in ghosts, demons, or angels?" Grady asked nonchalantly.

Ethan was puzzled but decided to play along. "Well, I don't *dis*believe in them, but I've also never seen one."

"Fair enough." Grady scratched something out on his form. "Do you frequently experience *déjà vu*, hear disembodied voices, or converse with other species?"

Ethan scoffed. "Uh, no."

Grady raised a curious eyebrow at him as if he thought Ethan might be lying but then marked out a few more things on his form. Ethan tried to lean forward to see what they were but couldn't make anything out from his vantage point.

"I'm sorry, but what's the point of these questions?" Ethan interrupted, growing impatient.

"I need to figure out exactly how you'll fit in here," Grady explained in a matter-of-fact manner. "What I really need to discern is what makes you *special*."

Finally. A question Ethan found comfortable answering.

"Nothing," he responded confidently. He'd had quite enough of the odd doctor and his weird patient interview. "I'm sorry for wasting your time. I know this will be a huge disappointment to Arthur since he wanted me to meet with you so badly. But I'm not special. I'm the opposite of that."

"Oh? How so?" Grady prodded, apparently engaged by Ethan's testy tone.

"Look, I may have these psychotic dream episodes every day, but I still go to school. I still fulfill obligations and responsibilities. I've got my shit handled." Ethan caught himself, hoping he didn't offend the doctor with his language.

Grady seemed unfazed, so he continued.

"I don't usually run to people with my problems like I did today. Which I now kind of regret," Ethan admitted.

"Although...I guess it was worth it just to see your cool office. By the way, were those tarot cards out there?"

"Yes," Grady confirmed. His interest seemed piqued.

Inexplicably flustered, Ethan continued his rant. "Anyway, the point is I'm fine. I'm not special or in need of any help. I don't even know why I came here. I'm just weird and...I'm fine with that. No big deal."

He grabbed his bag to leave when Grady surprised him.

"You're hired."

Ethan froze. *What?*

"What?" he echoed himself aloud, perplexed.

"You seem like a confident and resilient young man. Your talents could be strengthened with proper training, which I, of course, will provide. You will, however, need to work on your temperament, but as you saw with Vivian, that can be done during the course of your employment. I understand it's not something that can change about a person overnight. Sadly," Grady conceded, as if he'd spent many years trying to figure out a way to do just that. "Overall, I believe Arthur was right. You'd be a great intern here."

Ethan was overwhelmed with confusion.

"This...this was a *job interview*?" He wasn't sure if he should continue his upward motion or sit down. He had kind of stopped moving in the middle of standing up.

"Yes. And I think it went very well." Grady beamed as he sauntered around the desk to pat Ethan on the shoulder in a warm welcome.

Ethan collapsed into the chair, dumbfounded, as he processed what had happened.

Grady leaned back to prop himself on his desk and crossed his arms to stare down at Ethan. Now he was the one who seemed bewildered. "Why on earth did you think you were here?"

Three: The Mysterious Dr. Grady Hunter

"YOU TRICKED ME!" Ethan accused through the phone as he walked home from his surprise interview.

"I beg your pardon?" Arthur pretended not to understand the context of Ethan's statement, but his voice gave him away as he was clearly amused.

"A job interview! Really?" In truth, Ethan was only mildly frustrated with Arthur at this point, but he enjoyed chiding him anyway.

"Oh *that*. Did it not go well?"

"Apparently, it went great." Ethan shifted his dark-brown leather messenger bag on his shoulder as he crossed to the next street. The air was cool and crisp as autumn had arrived. It was starting to get dark, so he picked up his pace. His apartment wasn't too far from Grady's office, but he didn't like being out once the sun set. It always made him uneasy as if he were being watched. He was sure his paranoia was irrational, but he didn't have the patience at the moment to be rational.

"I'm now an intern for a doctor who I'm not even sure specializes in any real medical field."

"That's great news! Congratulations!"

"Seriously, though, what's with all the new-age Marie Laveau stuff there? It's worse than your office at the university." His keys jingled as he pulled them out of his pocket once he rounded the corner to his complex. "Ouija boards, tarot cards...not to mention, it smelled like a head shop with the amount of incense they'd been burning. What is he, some upscale witch doctor or something?"

Arthur let out a hearty laugh as if Ethan had told the best joke he'd heard all week. "He's eccentric, I'll give you that."

"Yeah, well, so are his employees," Ethan said, remembering the aloof secretary and peculiar office assistant, as he entered his small apartment and locked the door. He threw his bag on the ground and went to the kitchen for a glass of water.

"The people who work there seem so weird."

"And now you're one of them," Arthur proclaimed as though it were something to be proud of.

"Yeah, about that... I'm not sure I'm actually going back yet." Ethan took a drink. But he was lying. The truth was, the whole ordeal had left him with nothing but excitement and intrigue. Even if he didn't end up keeping the job, his curiosity had gotten the best of him and he definitely planned on showing up tomorrow evening as Grady had asked. He wasn't going to let Arthur off the hook easily, however, so he was playing coy.

"Sometimes, Ethan, the right doors open at the right times, and it would be terribly remiss not to go through them," Arthur said, his voice quiet and kind.

Ethan rolled his eyes and sat down on a barstool in his kitchen. He then fixed his gaze on the ceiling fan as he thought. He could tell Arthur was keeping something from him. There was a reason he'd set this whole thing up, but if he wasn't openly offering answers, Ethan had known him long enough to realize he'd have to be patient and find out.

The blades of the fan circled so fast that he was practically hypnotized by them as reality slipped away, and he lost himself in thought

"Hello?" Arthur prompted.

"Sorry," Ethan replied. "I'm just tired."

"Better get some rest then. I have a feeling you'll need all the energy you can muster tomorrow."

"Oh, yeah? How's that?" Ethan slid off the stool and moved to his worn-out couch to lie down. It was uncharacteristically frilly and floral compared to the rest of his apartment, but that was because he'd inherited it from his mother when he moved out earlier that year.

"First day at a new job."

"Yeah, I guess," Ethan mumbled. Then he decided to ask his question despite knowing he wouldn't get a straight answer. "So, why did you send me there, Arthur? Really."

Arthur paused a moment as if considering what he wanted to divulge. "I feel like it's the right path for you. The right door. I was waiting for you to be ready for the opportunity and push the door open on your own."

Once again. No real answer. Just riddles. Just like Arthur.

"All right then, my white rabbit. Have a good evening." Ethan hung up. He let his phone drop to the floor and closed his eyes, intending to take a short rest. He still had a project to finish for his history class and he couldn't afford a bad grade. He was sure Dr. Wallace would have his eye on him after his recent disruptive outburst.

Despite this, he fell into a deep sleep which lasted through the night. For the first time in years, there weren't any nightmares to wake him.

"CRAP!" ETHAN JUMPED up, realizing he'd slept into the next day. His window blinds were left open and the sun glared down on him. The clock above his television seemed to tick with disapproval as he noticed he'd missed his first class, not to mention his unfinished project.

He ran to change clothes and brush his teeth and hair. Then, instead of grabbing his bag and heading out, he sat down on the couch and recalled everything that had happened the evening before and was thrilled to have not had any bad dreams for once. His first instinct was to text Arthur and let him know, but he stopped himself. If he did, then Arthur would expect to see him on campus later, and Ethan quickly decided he didn't want to go there today.

Who could focus when they were going to be starting a job with a witch doctor who hailed from across the pond? Nope, there would be no school today. Ethan would spend the day doing his own research on Grady. *What exactly is he a doctor of, anyway?*

Ethan made some strawberry Pop-Tarts and a dark-roast coffee and then sat down at his laptop to summon the most powerful resource of knowledge he had: Google.

Surprisingly, Google was not of any help when it came to Dr. Grady Hunter. His office didn't have a website, he didn't use social media, and there weren't even any pictures of him in the image search. The single piece of evidence that he even existed was a written piece from the *Shady Pines Gazette* three years ago. He'd been interviewed at the grand opening of Aphrodite's Love Parlour, an adult store, that had since gone out of business due to the community's distaste with its location three doors down from the oldest church in town. The student population of the university had kept it afloat for a while, but business quickly dwindled as the owner received a reputation for being rude and hostile toward customers. Or so Ethan had heard. He'd never actually been there. Now the building housed a comic book and gaming shop. The article identified him as "a local alternative healer," and quoted him: *"I'm excited for this shop and the owner. I think it'll be a fantastic addition to our downtown area and generate an abundance of interest in the neighborhood."*

Ethan tried to imagine Grady, the poised British gentleman who he'd met yesterday, at the kinky store, grinning and giving it a big thumbs-up. He laughed to himself.

However, that was it. Nothing more on the mysterious Dr. Hunter, and the one thing he did find only made him more of an enigma to Ethan.

Ethan searched alternative healers and medicines and such, but it all seemed so cheesy. *How can anyone buy into this stuff?* People most certainly did, though, because Grady seemed to be able to afford a lot of expensive oddities and antiquities he'd peppered throughout his office. Ethan could only imagine how his home must be decorated.

After getting sucked into the time-stealing vortex of the internet, Ethan realized he only had an hour before Grady expected him to show up for work. He took a quick shower, ate a microwaved dinner, and then proceeded to spend more time than necessary obsessing over what to wear for his first day as a new-age healing intern. *Whatever that is.*

Grady had dressed like he'd stepped off the pages of *GQ,* but Benny had been so casual. Ethan frowned, riffling through his tiny closet space. There must not be a dress code or else Grady would have informed him, so Ethan grabbed something he thought was practical and comfortable. He pulled on a pair of clean jeans, which was kind of a big deal since he would usually wear the same pair for two weeks before worrying about washing them. He put on a black shirt with white sketched lines emulating a broken checkerboard pattern and slipped on some black oxfords he usually only wore to family occasions. He made a mental note to ask Grady if he could wear sneakers in the future. If he decided to keep the job, that is.

He quickly headed out and made it to Grady's office precisely at 6:00 p.m. as requested.

As soon as he entered the doors of the office, he was hit with both the overpowering smell of frankincense and the force of Benny pouncing on him in a giant and unexpected embrace.

"Ethan's here!" Benny announced excitedly as he released Ethan from the bear hug.

"Benny!" Vivian scolded as she stood up at her desk. "What did we say about personal space?"

"Sorry!" He quickly took two giant steps backward.

"Uh, it's okay," Ethan said politely. Although, it was extremely uncomfortable to be greeted by a new coworker with such enthusiasm. He tried not to seem too shocked.

Benny beamed, minding his distance. "Grady told me all about you. I've never got to train anyone before. This will be so much fun!"

With a little hop in his step, Benny led Ethan to the front desk and leaned on a box of files Vivian had placed there moments before.

Ethan tried not to sound too disappointed. "I thought Grady would be training me."

"He's very busy." Vivian crossed her arms and appraised him. "You probably won't see much of him tonight."

"A lot of people go to the doctor from four to midnight?" Ethan had noted the office's strange business hours, but thankfully they fit in with his class schedule. He just had to make sure to actually wake on time.

Vivian nodded, as if it were a silly thing to ask. "Oh yes. Most of our clients don't go out during the day. We're also especially busy before a full moon."

Ethan glanced at Grady's office door, which was now shut. He wondered if one of these "clients" was in there now.

"What exactly does he do?" Ethan asked. "Is he in there aligning chakras or giving crystal therapy or something?"

Vivian glared at him like he was dense. Her tone then became extremely condescending, even more so than usual.

"Grady is a supernatural healer. He takes on all kinds of roles, though, not only healing. He also does therapy, exorcisms, and hex-reversal. Right now, for instance, he's on the phone with a vampire from London, giving advice on the expulsion of a soul that's tethered itself to an antique Victrola. Every time the vampire tries to play one of his favorite albums, the spirit starts howling like a banshee and flings the record across the room, breaking anything in its path. It's spoiled two parties already, and that's two spoiled parties too many for any self-respecting vampire."

Ethan blinked slowly at Vivian and then laughed harder than he had in a long time. "You had me going there for a second. I thought you were serious."

Vivian frowned at him in disapproval.

"Really! He's amazing!" Benny said, taking over. "He can connect you to the spirits of your loved ones. He can calm melodramatic poltergeists... Once, he even helped a hobgoblin dispel a bout of hiccups he'd had for three decades. Grady is the best. He's a jerk of all trades."

"Jack," Vivian corrected.

"No, Grady. Who's Jack?" Benny raised a confused eyebrow.

"*Hobgoblin*?" Ethan appraised them both earnestly and realized they were deadly serious. "Are you saying you really believe in this stuff? It's parlor tricks, you know."

"I think Grady is making a mistake," she snapped at Benny. Vivian shot Ethan a contemptuous glare and then excused herself from the room.

As she walked out, Benny's face fell, but he tried to smooth things over. "Sorry about that. She's really serious about her job. And Grady. And life. And everything in the general realm of existence, actually."

"I didn't mean to upset her. I mean…none of that stuff is real, so it's weird to talk about it like it is."

Benny cocked his head quizzically to one side as if he were trying to make a decision.

"You guys really believe this stuff," stated Ethan. It wasn't a question this time. He realized he was definitely in the company of crazy people. Not like he hadn't had enough warning to this point.

Benny's gaze then flickered over Ethan's shoulder and his animated smile returned.

"There's no better way to make a believer than to have the evidence at hand," he said, nodding in gesture to the entrance.

Ethan glanced over his shoulder in time to see a man walk through the door. Literally, through the door. A noncorporeal form glided in through the glass and made itself at home on the same chair Ethan had sat on when he'd arrived to meet Grady yesterday. It didn't acknowledge them as it patiently and quietly waited.

Ethan turned to Benny in shock. "Is that…a *ghost*?"

Benny grinned delightedly and shoved Ethan lightly on the shoulder. "Hooray! We have a believer. Now all that's left is the training."

Four: House Call

TRAINING WASN'T AT all what Ethan had hoped it would be. There were no crystal balls involved. He wasn't learning spells, and he wasn't getting to help exorcise demons any time soon. It was actually the typical mundane tasks any office had. Organizing files, updating information, and learning what codes meant what on patient charts. Vivian had also been right. Ethan hadn't seen Grady once the entire time since he'd been stuck in the back offices with Benny.

The only bit of excitement in the past few hours had been right before his break when Benny had accidentally bumped into a filing cabinet and knocked over an urn full of grave dirt. He'd panicked, proclaiming it was horribly bad luck and Grady would be extremely upset. He asked Ethan to help clean it up and never let anyone know it'd happened. Beyond that fiasco, the evening had remained quite dull.

Once he returned from his break, which he'd taken down the street at a diner, Ethan found the dynamic had shifted. Both Vivian and Benny were deeply concerned when he walked in, and Grady was throwing on a crimson-red scarf and sepia-brown cabbie hat. His ill temper seemed to radiate around the room, and Ethan wondered if he'd found out about the grave dirt.

When Grady saw Ethan arrive, he turned to face him. "Ah, perfect timing. I need you to come with me on a house call."

Ethan's heart plummeted. This was the moment he'd been waiting for all day, but now that it was here, he suddenly had the urge to run all the way home to his apartment and pretend none of this had ever happened.

"You're taking him with you?" Vivian protested. She glanced at Ethan warily. However, this time, her eyes didn't seem angry but rather concerned.

"He'll be fine. I'll make sure of it."

"Fine?" Ethan asked. "Where are we going?"

"There are rumors an old frie...*acquaintance* of mine is conjuring unwelcome guests," Grady explained as he moved toward the door. "I need to check in and see if there's any truth to it."

"Conjuring?" Ethan gulped. "Are...are you saying we're going to see a witch?"

"Is that a problem? You've been working with a witch all evening, and it hasn't seemed to bother you so far."

Perplexed, Ethan turned to Benny. Benny shook his head and motioned with his thumb at Vivian. She winked at Ethan and produced a smug smile.

"Oh..." Ethan's vocabulary had completely left him.

"We're wasting time. I'd prefer to deal with this and leave before eleven," Grady said.

"What happens at eleven?" Ethan asked as they headed out.

"Do you only speak in questions? I'm not Alex Trebek," Grady said as they approached his maroon Jaguar.

"No...I..." Ethan attempted to answer but couldn't think of anything witty. So as he got in on the passenger side, he repeated, "What happens at eleven?"

Grady sighed as he started the car. "She gets tricky."

"SO IS SHE a wicked witch?" Ethan joked as they pulled in front of a small and rundown shop. There were palmistry paintings on the building and a sign that read *Fortune Teller*. Ethan considered it very kitschy.

"I wonder, Ethan... If you were on the edge of a volcano and I told you to close your eyes, jump in, and I would save you...would you do it?" Grady asked. He turned off the car and stared calculatingly at the building.

"What? No. That's crazy," responded Ethan with a laugh.

"Either you have nothing but blind faith in me or you don't understand the gravity of the situation. I believe it's the latter." Grady turned to face Ethan. His expression was full of contemplation.

"Are you saying she could hurt me?" Ethan's heart pounded more with nervousness than the excitement that had been there a moment before.

"The only person Marguerite can hurt is me, and that's because I let her," Grady assured him, checking his rearview mirror as if he thought they might be being followed.

Ethan sighed in exasperation. "Then what are you talking about, Grady? Seriously! I have been nothing but perpetually confused from the moment I met you." Ethan sighed in exasperation.

"I'm quite alluring that way, aren't I?" This time, it was Grady who was being playful as he flashed a charming smile and winked at Ethan.

"Yes, actually." Ethan laughed. He figured it was pointless to deny the fact. He'd done nothing but ponder about Grady for the past twenty-four hours. "But really, what's going on?"

"Ethan, there will come a time when you'll look back on this moment and hate me for it. You'll probably think it was foolish of me to bring you here, and you might be right. But I run on my own blind faith. The belief we can never overcome our demons unless we face them head-on."

Ethan thought he sounded like a poet, but he decided that was probably because he had a British accent and a fancy scarf on.

"So, is Marguerite your demon? Is she your ex-girlfriend or something?"

"No. I don't date women. Not anymore. And she's not my demon. Just a pain in my ass."

"You're making a really big deal about this. Are you sure it's safe for me to go in there?" Ethan stared at the fortune teller's building again. It was pitch-black out with nothing but a foreboding waxing moon to highlight the worried creases of his brow.

Grady reached over Ethan's knees to pop open the glove box and took out a small vial of oil.

"Don't let fear of the unknown stop you now. Here," Grady offered. "If you're worried, then unbutton your shirt."

"Excuse me?" Ethan's cheeks flushed in embarrassment and confusion at Grady's request. He stared at the vial, perplexed.

"Your shirt. Unbutton it," Grady instructed. "I may not be a witch myself, but I've learned a few tricks over the years."

Ethan wasn't sure why he seemed so comfortable with Grady or why he did everything he asked without much question. Perhaps it was his charismatic personality and good looks or his confidence that made Ethan assume Grady always knew best. Whatever it was, he was sitting in his new boss's car, in the dark, unbuttoning his shirt. *Not telling Arthur about this. Nope. Never.*

It wasn't as awkward as Ethan had imagined. Grady produced a drop of oil onto his fingertip and drew onto his chest a symbol Ethan couldn't discern.

"*Tueri hoc corpus a nocentibus,*" Grady said as he drew the symbol on. "There. That will help ward off anything she might try to do."

"Was that Latin? That will really work?"

"It will if you don't sweat too much."

"Sounds kind of ineffective," Ethan mused as he buttoned his shirt.

"In truth, no magic is ever completely effective," Grady conceded as they exited the car.

Ethan frowned thoughtfully. "That's disappointing."

"Trust me. It's a blessing. Don't ever feel invincible because you're not. Just know, neither are they," Grady said as they walked toward Marguerite's shop.

"Who?"

"Everyone."

"MORE TAROT CARDS," Ethan declared as they walked inside. The door was unlocked, so they had let themselves in. Ethan had spotted the deck immediately. They lay out as if it had been recently used on a nearby table. He also noted the familiar scent of incense that seemed so favored by this crowd.

"I'm going to have to get a set someday. They seem pretty popular," he added, leaning to study the cards more closely.

"I've found they're both useful and tedious depending on the user." Grady seemed to only be partially paying attention to Ethan's amusement with the shop, busy scanning the place for signs of its owner.

He didn't have to search for long. She quickly emerged from a room in the back.

"Grady! To what do I owe the pleasure of your visit?" Marguerite leaned her slim but curvy frame against a nearby cabinet, which contained a collection of crystals and oils for sale. Her long strawberry-blonde hair cascaded over her shoulders, framing her chest, which was barely contained in the dark-blue bohemian day dress she had cinched in a brown leather corset. Her eyes sparkled a gorgeous blue, and Ethan was too shy to face her directly. Though, he did note she was eying him quite openly.

"The pleasure is all yours, I assure you," Grady said curtly. "And I suppose you owe it to whatever seedy character you've been doling out information to recently."

She frowned at his cold greeting and walked to the other side of the cabinet to pretend to straighten a shelf of ceremonial daggers.

"You'll have to be more specific. I give information to lots of people," she replied with a decidedly naive tone. "The whole town comes to hear what I can tell them about their lives."

"Don't flatter yourself." Grady rolled his eyes. "Business isn't that good for you, and we both know it."

"Fine," she snapped, then put on a bright and seductive smile. "Why are you here and who's your cute friend?"

"I'm—" Ethan started, but Grady quickly cut in.

"Of no concern to you. He's a new employee. I'm showing him the ropes."

"To hang himself with, I'm sure." All of Marguerite's faux friendliness disappeared. She crossed her arms and stood her ground, indicating she was done with their presence.

"There are rumors you've been contacted by someone. Something. Recently," Grady explained. "Apparently, you shared some personal information about me."

"Oh that." Marguerite rolled her eyes and shook her head as if it was nothing. "Who's tattletaling on me now? No worries. He wasn't really concerned with you."

"What did he want?" Grady demanded. Ethan glanced at him, wondering if Grady had never heard of the phrase *you can catch more flies with honey*. Ethan thought Grady's tone with Marguerite was harsh, but it was nothing compared to the expression on his face as he talked to her.

"I don't see how that's any of your business," she spat.

Grady pointed his index finger at her as if she were a petulant child. "Stop playing games, Marguerite! You are to have no further contact with this creature! Do I make myself clear?"

"Who are you to tell me what I can and can't do?" she exploded, taking great angry strides toward them. In response, Ethan shrunk behind Grady two steps.

"I think you're forgetting who has the upper hand here," Marguerite said with a devious smile. "Or did you stop worrying about how to fix Benny now that you have a new pet?" She pointed to Ethan.

"I can tell you have a protection spell on him. Were you worried I'd play with him too?"

"Do not speak to me of Benny unless you're ready to put things right!" The muscles in Grady's jaw flexed and Ethan thought again about running out the door.

"Things are as they should be, and don't piss me off or I'll give your new friend a similar fate," Marguerite shouted, and with a flick of her hand, she levitated a scrying ball off a table and hurled it at them. Grady grabbed Ethan's shoulders and the two ducked down as it flew overhead to smash into pieces on the wall behind them. Grady was back up just as quickly as if it wasn't the first time he'd dodged flying items Marguerite threw at him.

"You may twist lives but you do not control fate. I am warning you it would be very unwise, even for you, to contact this creature again," Grady said firmly. His expression shifted to something softer. "He'll not spare any life; including yours."

She seemed to back down as well as she stared him dead in the eye as if deciding whether or not to trust his words.

"Fine," she finally said. She walked to the table with the cards and sat down in one of the chairs.

"I wasn't really planning on talking to him again anyway, if you must know." She shook her head, gathered the cards, shuffled them, and started laying them out again. "I don't like it when you think you can tell me what to do."

"We both know that I can't," Grady said, placating her. "But I will always try to help you do what's right."

"Whatever, Grady." She sighed. "Look, he was just asking for me to help him find some key. He didn't really give any details. Anyway, I'm kind of busy at the moment so you can show yourself out."

"Contact me if you learn anything else." Grady didn't give her a second glance as he turned to leave.

"Yeah, sure," she mumbled, making it a point not to look at him either. She turned the cards over as Grady exited, leaving Ethan standing awkwardly between Marguerite and the door.

Ethan turned to follow, but Marguerite beckoned to him.

"Hey, kid." She was frowning at the cards in front of her.

"Watch your back," she said flatly as her eyes met his. For a brief second, he thought he saw tears, but she quickly returned to the cards, and he let himself out. Ethan waited until they were in the car to break the silence.

"What was that all about?" Ethan peeked into his shirt collar to try to tell if he'd sweat too much or not.

"Long story."

"Which part?"

"All of it."

"She told me to watch my back. You think she's going to come after me?" This time, Ethan was the one checking the rearview mirror to see if they were being followed.

"I think she knows that someone is," Grady confirmed.

"What? Why? Because I'm hanging out with you?" Ethan panicked. Nothing about today had turned out how he'd thought it would, and he got the feeling he was the only one that was in the dark about what was going on.

"Trust me, Ethan. The only thing keeping you safe is that you're *hanging out* with me." Grady said sternly as they turned on to a less traveled road. Ethan was pretty sure this wasn't the way to Grady's office.

"What is that supposed to mean? What's going on?" he asked his billionth question of the day. "And what about Benny? Did something happen to him? This is freaking me out." He shook his head at how stupid he'd been to jump blindly into all of this. He fumbled around for his phone so he could call Arthur to come pick him up.

"Marguerite and I used to be friends," Grady answered softly. Ethan stopped searching for his phone. Was he finally going to get a real answer? He calmed down a little and relaxed in his seat to listen.

"She used to work for me, I saw so much potential in her."

"As a witch?" Ethan asked, wondering if Grady also saw potential in Vivian.

"As a person," Grady corrected. "To live a regular life and do *normal* things. I helped teach her how to live a life without magic. I even helped her open her own business."

"The tarot shop?"

"No. It was an adult entertainment shop." Grady chuckled. "Which was a poor choice, but I wasn't going to argue since I was happy she'd at least chosen something that didn't have to do with magic." Grady's eyes creased with amusement as he spoke. He had the faraway expression of someone envisioning fond memories. Then it was gone. He was aware of Ethan again.

"It fit her personality, but I was slowly seeing a change in her." They turned down another road Ethan didn't recognize.

"Wait. Marguerite was the lady from Aphrodite's Love Parlour?" Now Ethan was the one wearing amusement on his face.

"You knew that place?" Grady smiled and glanced expectantly at Ethan.

"No. Not really." Ethan blushed. "Just read about it online."

"You googled me," said Grady, seeming rather pleased with himself.

"What? No!" Even Ethan didn't believe his own protest, so he didn't fight away the telling smile set across his face. He was growing comfortable with Grady, like an old friend. Or rather a new friend that would one day be an old friend. He'd also already forgotten about calling Arthur to save him.

"It's the only bit of information about me on the internet." Grady shrugged. "You think I haven't googled myself? Everyone does."

"Yeah, why is that anyway?"

"Narcissism. Obviously."

Ethan was pretty sure they weren't in the main part of town anymore.

"No. I mean, why isn't there any information about you?" Ethan covertly glanced around searching for road signs.

"Because I don't exist," answered Grady.

Ethan turned to him in shock. "You're a ghost too?"

"What?" Grady's nose scrunched in a mix of bemusement and disgust. "No, *M. Night Shyamalan.*"

Ethan recovered from his inaccurate revelation and stopped wondering how a ghost could apply cologne, run a business, and drive a car. Not to mention apply oily wards to his employee's chests.

"My name isn't Grady Hunter. And FYI, I'm not a real doctor." Grady grinned as if he'd let the world's fattest cat out of its smallest bag.

"I kind of guessed that last part." It was Ethan's turn to roll his eyes. "What's your real name?"

"I *was* telling a story."

"Sorry. Go on."

"By teaching Marguerite to ignore her powers, I had inadvertently been creating a monster. She became more angry and disenchanted with the world every day," Grady continued.

"Well, yeah. You made her be someone she wasn't."

"Yes." Grady sighed. "It's not so easy to see when you're living it."

"She's back to full witch now, so why is she still full bitch?" Ethan smirked at his own joke.

"You're not actually that funny, you know."

"Sorry." Ethan cringed a little and bit his lip. Even if they'd achieved some sort of friend status, Grady still made him insanely nervous.

"I ruined her," Grady continued. "She thought I loved her. She did everything I asked and I did nothing but tell her to be something she's not. And I continue to, even today. The truth is, I thought I saw something good in her, but...it was never there. She was passionate and beautiful but a void of nothingness when it came to compassion or empathy."

"That's...sad."

The car became too quiet.

"And Benny?" Ethan asked, partially out of genuine curiosity and partially to break the silence.

"I'll let him tell you that part of the story when he's ready,"

"Thanks." Ethan sighed, letting his head lean onto the headrest. He'd finally realized they were heading to a residential area slightly out of town. It was where a lot of the wealthier citizens lived. He assumed they must be following up on some other lead before they returned to the office.

"For what?"

"For finally telling me something real," Ethan answered, closing his eyes to embrace the darkness. He was incredibly sleepy.

"By the end, I'll have told you too much and then where will we be?" Grady's voice sounded sad. Ethan turned his attention to the road in time for a huge mass of dark fur with glowing amber eyes to collide with their vehicle.

It slammed into the side of them, and the car went spinning and rolled into a ditch. When Ethan opened his eyes, he was hanging upside down and Grady was gone.

Five: Wolves Walk in Darkness, but Men Walk in Shadow

THE WORLD WAS upside down. No. Ethan was upside down. It took him only a moment to realize the car had rolled over and he was hanging from his seat belt. He worried he'd been injured but, after a quick personal inspection, seemed to have, thankfully, remained mostly intact.

Grady was missing. Had he been thrown out? The driver's side window had been rolled down, and Ethan moved to test his own to see if it would work. Success.

He unlatched his seat belt and carefully positioned himself so he could crawl out of the car. He met the cold earth of the ditch with his outstretched hands and slowly pulled himself up. He couldn't see anything. It was too dark and a mist had accumulated around him. The headlights of the car and the moon gave the only light as he scanned the scene.

"Grady?" he asked the empty air.

There was no response. Had he been injured? Had he gone for help?

"Grady!" Ethan shouted.

Still nothing.

Then the crack of steps sounded on the ground behind him. He wheeled around, but no one was there.

"Grady!" Ethan called out in the direction of the noise. He needed him to make another sound so he could find him and help him. Again, there was no answer.

He fumbled around in his pocket for his phone to call for help, but unfortunately, that too was missing.

"Grady! Can you hear me?" He listened intently for any response.

"No one can hear you here," a gravelly voice growled out from the darkness in front of him. It sounded both sinister and amused.

Ethan's heart plummeted as a cold chill ran up his spine. He took a shaky step toward the car. Sounds of movement rushed toward him.

"Look out," a voice shouted, but before Ethan had time to react, a young woman flung herself at him, knocking him to the ground a few paces away. At the same moment, a giant black-haired wolf leaped at him but missed, thanks to the girl's quick action.

She was on her feet in moments, facing the monster. Ethan stared up with wide-eyed shock. It was the girl from his dreams. Her fiery red hair glistened, and for a moment, he thought it might actually be sparkling but quickly realized it was glistening from the moonlight. The light also shone off something in her hand. She was wielding a knife.

The monster quickly recovered from his missed attack and lunged at her with snarling and snapping fangs.

She wasted no time stabbing the beast in the eye with the knife.

The creature howled in pain and stood to full height. It was taller than Ethan had realized, at least eight feet in height. It backed away, pawing at its wound in anger.

The girl pivoted on her heel to face Ethan, who had just barely stood, in awe of what he'd witnessed.

"You have to go!" she implored.

Ethan glanced around helplessly. He had no idea where the road led or what other horrific creatures might be out in the dense darkness of the night.

"Go? Go where?" he asked, throwing his hands up in terrified exasperation.

The girl cocked an eyebrow at him and then glanced back to see the wolf refocusing his attention on them.

"You still don't know?"

Ethan let out a disheartened laugh. "I don't know anything anymore!"

"You have to wake up," she instructed, nodding at him with conviction.

"W-wake up?" Ethan repeated her words and only then did he realize he had been dreaming.

"Wake up," she shouted at him.

"Wake up," another voice chimed in.

"Wake up!" The voices coaxed him together until the girl's voice faded away and only one remained. The earnestly pleading voice of Grady.

"Ethan, wake up!" Grady was shaking Ethan by the shoulders when he finally opened his eyes.

Ethan sat forward, suddenly alert, his chest heaving with the rush of adrenaline.

Grady sighed with relief. "Are you all right?"

Ethan tried to catch his breath and gather himself. It mortified him that Grady had witnessed one of his episodes, but even more so, he was terrified it might all still be happening. His eyes darted around, and he quickly assessed they were sitting in Grady's unharmed vehicle and none of the events he'd experienced had actually transpired. In fact, they were parked in front of a stone two-story house outside of town, and the motor of the car was humming mundanely as if even it were wondering what Ethan's problem was.

Ethan closed his eyes, took a deep calming breath, and shook his head to both reassure himself he was awake now and let Grady know even he recognized how crazy he must seem.

"Are you...all right?" Grady repeated.

"I—I must have fallen asleep on the drive," Ethan stammered.

"What happened?" Grady asked, taking a handkerchief out of his pocket.

Ethan wondered if anyone in the world besides elderly men and Grady actually still carried handkerchiefs in their pockets. He was distracting himself. It was his way of dealing with his own madness. Redirection and distraction.

"It was a nightmare," Ethan reassured him. "Like the ones I told you about. Just...worse than ever."

Grady ran the handkerchief along Ethan's forehead and then held it out for him to see.

"I'll say. Just a dream?" Grady showed him the handkerchief—it was covered in blood.

"That's impossible," Ethan said. He shook his head, fighting off any notions that might have been forming. "I must have scratched myself or something. Really. It's no big deal. I'm so sorry. See. *This* is why Arthur told you about me. I do have issues."

Grady put the handkerchief away calmly and turned off the car.

"Don't be embarrassed. I can tell you're nervous around me. You don't have to be," Grady said soothingly. "Maybe I *can* help."

"Even if I'm not a witch or a ghost or a vampire?" Ethan quipped.

Grady smiled. "Especially because you're not any of those things."

"Yeah, okay," Ethan agreed. "And how are you going to do that?"

"First, I'm going to invite you into my home and give you a nice hot cup of tea. You look like a man who could use an infusion of lemon balm and lavender."

"At this point, I'll try anything." Ethan followed Grady's lead in exiting the vehicle. He hesitated momentarily, checking to see if anything was prowling in the night around them. But with Grady by his side, he found the courage to walk the long drive toward the stone house. His attention focused on the new information before him. This was where Grady lived. Ethan wondered how many times Arthur must have already visited and exactly how long they'd known each other after all. Was it a new friendship? Or had Grady existed silently in the shadows of Arthur's life the entire time?

Grady's home was extremely large and the gravel drive that led to it was lined by Victorian-era streetlamps that warmly lit the walk to the entryway. The gray-stone house appeared to be built in the late 1800s, which was standard for the houses outside their town. Most of them were old farmhouses. Ethan thought the structure suited Grady well. It was a beautiful home that maintained a sense of old-world dignity and mystery, not unlike its owner.

"You live here all by yourself?" Ethan asked aloud and then internally wondered if the connotations of that question were rude.

"I'm not entirely alone," Grady vaguely answered as the doors opened inexplicably of their own accord, as if the house were expecting them.

Six: Friendship in C Minor Sharp

GRADY'S HOME WAS warm and welcoming once they stepped inside. He had obviously carefully curated every corner with Georgian décor and design to match the exterior of the old house. Although, Ethan had to wonder if maybe some of the items had been there far before Grady. Perhaps he'd inherited it. There was still so much to learn about him.

As the doors shut behind them and Grady hung his hat, scarf, and jacket on a nearby brass rack, a little dog came scuttling into the entryway, barking with enthusiasm.

"Cute dog." Ethan kneeled down to greet the little tan Chihuahua as it sniffed and licked his hands. Its tail waged war on the air around it with the most energized wagging one could coax from a canine.

"Oh, that's just Benny," Grady said, resting his hands on his hips as he watched the two bond.

Ethan scrutinized him. "You named your dog after your employee?"

"Technically, the dog came first." Grady shrugged. He was then distracted by a figure who had appeared in the room. It was half the form of a middle-aged woman. She wore an Edwardian-era dress and her hair was swept into a bun. However, she was translucent and floated nearby them.

"Good evening, Agatha," Grady greeted the specter. "Would you mind fetching some tea for us? Lemon balm and lavender, please."

Agatha had been staring at Ethan, but she nodded to Grady upon his request and flew from the room.

"Your house is haunted?"

The Chihuahua headed out of the room as well, following in the direction of the ghostly woman.

"Former owners. The husband is around here, too, somewhere. Usually in the kitchen."

"And now they take orders from you? That must be weird. To die and then be servants in your own home," Ethan mused.

"When you say it like that, it makes me sound so horrid." Grady's nose crinkled in mild self-disgust. Then he shook it off. "I assure you, they're quite happy. They were floating around aimlessly when I arrived, and now they have a sense of purpose again. I let them stay, and they keep things running smoothly. It's the perfect arrangement."

Ethan gave a demure grin. "And it has nothing to do with the fact you charm your way into getting everyone to do exactly what you want them to?"

"You find me charming?" Ethan couldn't tell if he was being flirtatious or verbally backing him into a corner.

His cheeks burned. There was no retracting the statement because his face would only betray him. All that he managed was a quiet laugh of avoidance.

"I'm really good at reading people." Grady winked. "And *former* people." He gestured down the hall in the direction of his ghostly roommates.

"So, you're not supernatural then?" Ethan surmised. He'd been wondering it all night after everything he'd witnessed. "You don't have some gift for appealing to people in order to manipulate them? And you don't use a spell to coerce people?"

"Goodness, no! Do you feel like I've manipulated you somehow?" Grady seemed wounded. "My sincerest apologies. I thought we were getting along."

"We are!" Ethan quickly corrected. "I mean, I'm not... sorry, that all came out wrong. What I mean is, everyone seems to like you. I mean *really* like you. At least initially," he added, in regards to Marguerite. "Most people don't have that effect on everyone they meet."

"Well, I don't either. Not on everyone," Grady assured him. "And to answer your question, no. No spells. No supernatural powers. I'm simply, undoubtedly, human in every way."

"I really hope I didn't offend you." Ethan was flush with embarrassment.

"Ethan, you need to relax. You're very stiff," Grady said, placing a firm but warm grip upon Ethan's shoulders to let him know that all was well between them. "And you didn't offend me. I understand all of this"—he gestured around in general with one hand—"is a lot to take in."

Agatha returned with the tea.

"Ah, thank you," Grady said, taking the cups and handing one to Ethan. Agatha flew off again, disappearing through a wall.

Grady nodded for Ethan to follow him, and they headed down the hall and into a massive study. Grady guided him to two brown wingback chairs. They sat in front of a gold-trimmed fireplace that was already glowing with the warmth of flame. Ethan guessed this was Agatha's doing as well.

The room carried the same interior design as the rest of the house. The wallpaper was crimson damask, and all the trim was in hunter green, brass, and gold. There were paintings hung nearly everywhere, and more antique treasures, like the ones in his office, decorated the room.

Ethan thought he also spotted a collection of weaponry in the far corner and an antique grand piano behind them. It was as if he'd been transported to a different time or was in one of the BBC specials his mother liked to watch. Grady's accent only added to the ambiance.

"I have learned tricks over the years for combating the powers of others, though, as you witnessed tonight," Grady continued. "They're essential to know in my line of work."

"I'd love to learn that kind of stuff. It's pretty fantastic." Ethan took a sip of the tea. Grady was right; it seemed like what he'd needed.

"It's dark, it's lonely, and it's forever. That's what it is," Grady said, staring directly into the licking flames of fire before them as he also took a sip from his own cup.

"But you could teach me?"

"What part of anything I said sounded appealing to you?" Grady chuckled at Ethan's unwarranted enthusiasm.

"I get it. It's serious stuff, but...I never realized the possibilities before," Ethan explained. "That there's this entirely different world everyone turns a blind eye to every single day. We walk around obsessed with boring and trivial things without a clue that there's all of this potential and magic all around us."

Grady's face turned grim, and he appraised Ethan with an expression of pity. "You're twenty, correct?"

"Yeah..." Ethan answered, unsure of what his age had to do with anything.

"Three years older than I was the last time I viewed the world with a passionate eye like that," Grady said, but it was as if the words were meant to only be heard by himself.

"What happened?" Ethan set his cup down on a nearby table, gazing at Grady in earnest.

"The same thing that happened to you. I discovered there was more to our world."

"And that didn't thrill you?" Ethan was perplexed. He couldn't imagine feeling any other way but delighted and enthralled by his new reality.

"It made me the man I am today." Grady was staring at the fire again.

"But that's a good thing," Ethan countered, wanting to cheer Grady up. The man's eyes had grown dark and distant as if he were reliving a private moment in his mind. "You're the most interesting person I've ever met."

"Ethan, I'm a single thirty-seven-year-old ex-Brit living in the States under an alias with a Chihuahua as my only companion. I make a living off the unfortunate mishaps of the undead." Grady refocused on Ethan and smiled at him with sadness and a hint of whimsy. "And, yet, here you are telling me how great that all is."

"So you're one of *those* people." Ethan rolled his eyes.

"What people?" Grady arched his brow with interest.

"One of those people everyone else thinks is brilliant and amazing, but all you can see is the negative. You can't see past your perceived flaws, so you'll never understand why you're already perfect," Ethan stated with conviction.

"Trust me, I'm far from perfect."

"Well, you seem pretty close to me. I'd give anything to be you because as terrible as you seem to think your life is, at least you're not a twenty-year-old without prospects of a good future." Now it was Ethan's turn to share his self-pity. "The only people that care about me are my mom and Arthur, and I suspect Arthur only cares because he's had a crush on my mom forever. I'm earning a degree I'm not even sure I can do anything with. I'll probably end up single, too, because can you imagine anyone ever trying to sleep next to me? *Sorry, sweetheart, didn't mean to smack you in the face and scream like a banshee. I was being attacked by imaginary demons again.* I mean, really? Until I met you, I was going nowhere. Now...now, I think I might actually have a chance at doing something worthwhile. So yeah, sorry if it bothers you, but I think you're pretty amazing and I think the world suddenly is too." Ethan began to realize the truth of what he said as he spoke.

Grady studied him quietly and a brief moment of silence passed between the two. Then Grady seemed to pull himself out of whatever internal darkness he had spiraled into, and Ethan was triumphant he'd been able to reach through the man's mental veil and retrieve him.

"I know I hired you to work in my office with the others, but I suspect filing papers away with Benny might be a waste of your energy. I see so much potential in you to do brilliant things. At the risk of sounding cliché, I see a lot of my former self in you as well. Tell me, Ethan, would you be interested in being my apprentice?"

Ethan beamed. "Seriously? That would be amazing."

"Good. It's settled then." Grady took a deep breath, tacking on, "But if this is going to work, then you need to know who I *really* am."

"The man that came before Doctor Grady Hunter?" Ethan was definitely curious to find out more about that.

"There will come a time when I'll need you to trust me without question. It'll go against your better judgment, but it will be essential," Grady said. "For that to happen, you must know why the world, which you view as being full of endless possibility and wonder, is for me a void of painful darkness."

"What do you mean? What's going to happen?" Ethan sensed Grady slipping again, and it made him nervous.

"When you live amongst the supernatural, you quickly find there are few people you can trust and even fewer you can depend on. If we're to work alongside each other, we have to be able to trust one another wholly. Our lives will depend on it."

Ethan nodded in agreement, letting Grady know he was all in. "Okay."

Grady drank the last bit of tea from his cup, set it on the table next to Ethan's, and then leaned in his chair to face him.

"Growing up, my life was rather mundane. I was fine with that. I liked that. I was good at that. My father was an equestrian who trained horses, mostly in jumping, and I trained alongside him. That was to be my life, to follow in his footsteps." Grady's eyes flickered as he immersed himself in a memory again.

"One summer, there was this girl whose family hired us to train their horses. Being seventeen and mischievous, she and I would sneak off together regularly into the woods. She was beautiful, funny, and had the most compassionate heart I've ever known. We spent an entire summer exploring each other's hearts and falling in love. Then...I ruined everything."

A moment passed, and Ethan wondered if Grady was about to change his mind and end the story there, but he finally continued.

"I knew she was it for me. She was perfect. I decided to propose to her on the last day of summer. It felt right to end the perfect season with a new beginning together. I would take her out into the woods where we'd spent a lot of time under the trees, and in the moonlight, I would get down on my knee and make her mine forever. It was a gorgeous night with a full moon as the backdrop. I asked her to meet me there and..."

Ethan sensed things were about to take a bad turn. His heart tugged at Grady's story and for whatever was about to come next.

"I was running late because I hadn't told my family what I was up to. They didn't even realize we'd been meeting in secret the entire time. Or maybe they did, but they never mentioned it. So, when I was trying to go, my father kept giving me chores. I rushed through them, but when I finally finished, it was too late."

"She gave up on you?" Ethan asked quietly, assuming they never got to meet in the woods.

"No. I wish she would have...but no," Grady answered, almost breathless. "She waited for me, and when I finally arrived, it took a moment for the horror of what I was seeing to sink in. Her frame was lying sprawled on the ground by the tree where we'd first kissed. Her legs were...a few feet away. There was blood everywhere. I ran to her with my heart racing and tears stinging my eyes, screaming her name, *Ava!* And that's when he stepped out from the thick of the woods around us. This massive wolf, much taller than any man I'd ever met. He was surrounded by the stench of death, and his eyes were glistening with bloodlust. There was still fabric from her dress caught in his teeth. I was so full of fear. But it was offset by my pain and rage, and I pulled out a knife I kept inside my boot and I attacked him. It was the bravery of blind rage. I don't think he'd expected that reaction, and by catching him off guard, I was able to stab him in the abdomen. He fled into the trees and didn't return. I fell to my knees, and in that moment, I lost myself. She was the single most radiant being to ever grace my life and she was taken in an instant. She was my future. After that, there was nothing but darkness."

Grady finished, closing his eyes momentarily as though attempting to push the macabre memories back into the place in his mind and heart he'd accessed them from.

"I'm...I'm so sorry. That's terrible." Ethan wiped away the wetness from his eyes as he realized what a fool he must have sounded to Grady minutes before.

"That man doesn't exist anymore. I became someone else." Grady opened his eyes again. It was as if he were a phoenix, dying and being reborn each time he thought of her. "I knew no one would ever believe what had happened. I would obviously be blamed for a gruesome and violent murder. I had to leave."

"It was a werewolf, wasn't it?" Ethan stated more than questioned. He thought about the creature who had tried to attack him in his own dream earlier.

"I've spent my entire life since learning about the supernatural, training in the occult, immersing myself in the depths of darkness to destroy the damned and reform the soulless. I've taken my personal tragedy and turned it into a war. That is my life now. That is who I *really* am," Grady declared solemnly. "I'm afraid that I've become a menace myself and lost sight of things long ago...but I've also grown complacent with my actions."

"So...you've killed people?" Ethan asked but was unsure if he wanted to know the answer.

"I kill monsters...if they don't agree to reform their ways. But werewolves...yes, I kill them without blinking." Grady's brow was stubbornly furrowed in a way that told Ethan he'd had this argument many times before, probably with himself.

"But...werewolves are men. They're just cursed," Ethan reminded him softly.

"Werewolves are my enemy. He got away that night. I will not stop until I know every last one of their kind has been extinguished from existence. It's the only way I'll know her murderer met his fate at my hands." The words came from Grady as if he were reading aloud a manifesto. Ethan knew he shouldn't press the man anymore at this point. He had obviously set a chain of vengeance into motion two decades ago that would take a miracle to stop him from continuing.

"So, Ethan, do you still think I'm perfect?" Grady asked curtly, but his voice was resigned as he stared at the ceiling, waiting for whatever backlash was to come.

"No," Ethan answered honestly.

"You see the monster behind the mask now." Grady wore a self-deprecating smirk as if he expected Ethan would walk away at this point.

"I see someone who has been fighting a lonesome and weary war. Someone who has deep battle scars. I hope he can see he doesn't have to do it alone anymore." The words fell from Ethan's lips like a generous gift. He was offering the trust and loyalty Grady asked for. Grady's expression faltered as his words sunk in, and Ethan swore he glimpsed the man that used to exist twenty years before.

"You still want to work with me?"

"You said you think you might be able to help me. Well, I think I might be able to help you too. I think we both feel like we're living in our own personal freak show and maybe together we can find a way to remain somewhat human."

Grady sat straight in his chair and chuckled. It was as if the entire mood of the room had shifted, and in that moment, they knew they were connected somehow. "You said you didn't have any direction in life, but you seem to have a rather astute internal compass."

"I guess I meant that I didn't really see where I'd be going in the future." Ethan shrugged. "I mean, there's only one thing I've ever been even remotely good at."

"What's that?" This time it was Grady who seemed earnestly interested in finding out more about his new companion's past.

Ethan smiled coyly as he eyed the nearby piano. "I'll show you. The degree I'm working on...*was* working on, is in music."

Without a further word, Ethan sat down and rested his fingers on the familiar keys. Playing the piano was the only place he'd ever known a sense of calm and stability. Grady watched Ethan as he caressed the keys into playing a classic that was both haunting and rich in tone. Piano Sonata No. 14 in C Sharp Minor. Grady appeared mesmerized. Ethan could sense himself being studied with unwavering attention until he played the last note. He then turned to shrug modestly at Grady.

"Beethoven," Grady said wistfully. "Now *that* was perfect. You're rather surprising yourself."

"I'm glad you liked it. Do you play?"

"No." Grady shook his head. "I listen to a lot of classical music, though. It calms my nerves. Makes me a better roommate. Believe it or not, I used to come home and smash things after work. That is until Agatha suggested I put my emotions to better use and I picked up a paintbrush." He nodded to the paintings on the walls. They had looked so much like classic French Impressionist paintings Ethan had assumed they were also antiques.

"Those are amazing." Ethan complimented his artistry with genuine admiration. Then he peered at the actual antiques again.

"Where'd you get all this stuff, anyway? Do you really make that much money?" Ethan asked, wondering if they were good enough friends to ask such a prying question. He figured they were as Grady seemed unfazed by it.

"Most of my clients don't have money, so they pay me in antiquities. I keep what I like and sell the rest," he answered.

"That's really cool, actually... I'm sorry, but even after everything you said tonight, I still wish I were you." Ethan laughed, taking in the grandiose nature of the house again.

"Please don't. I wouldn't wish my life on anyone," Grady responded with a small polite smile.

"I think you turned out all right, considering." Ethan motioned his hands playfully as if he were weighing a scale.

Grady chuckled.

"I was thinking, you should stay the night here. It's late, and it might be good to err on the side of caution."

"I'm going to go out on a limb and guess you were thinking that the entire time. You did drive us here to begin with after all." Ethan smirked.

"Ah see, now that I've been honest, you can see right through me. I knew I'd regret that." Grady wagged his index finger at him in feigned disappointment.

Ethan laughed.

"Sure, why not?" He shrugged. "I'm sure you have a few rooms to spare here. Plus, my apartment feels...so far away now. More than in a measure of distance."

"Now that's a feeling I know too well. Make yourself at home. I'll go find Agatha and see that she prepares a room for you." Grady excused himself and left Ethan alone in the study.

Ethan carefully studied the impressive paintings as he waited, hoping one might offer even more insight about Grady. When the oils failed to offer up any further answers, the collection of weaponry caught his eye again, and he made his way to them. There were a couple of swords and small daggers but also a few knives all lined on a crimson satin cloth atop a desk. He thought about his nightmare again and how the girl had used a knife to defend him. He also thought about Grady's story and how a knife probably saved his life. Ethan decided maybe he should keep one close by tonight in case anything happened.

He stole a glance over his shoulder to make sure Grady hadn't returned yet. When he knew the coast was clear, he took one of the knives and slipped it into his back pocket, hidden beneath his shirt. He wasn't used to stealing things and the guilt quickly ate at him. He could probably ask Grady to borrow one, but he was afraid he would tell him he had nothing to fear at his house, and then he might be left defenseless again. So he decided to take the risk.

"This way," Grady said from the doorway. Ethan spun around, hoping Grady hadn't seen anything, but it seemed he'd not caught him.

Ethan followed Grady down the hallway, up a staircase, and into the guest bedroom that was to be his for the night. Unsurprisingly, it was similarly decorated. Except of course, for a very familiar object hanging above the four-poster bed.

The little Chihuahua, who had followed a few paces behind them, ran into the room and hopped onto the bed, excited at the prospect of having another human in the home to spend time with.

"A dream catcher? Did Arthur gift that to you? He's always trying to give them to me. I think they're his favorite thing to collect," Ethan teased.

"He's envious of mine because it actually works. He's been begging me for it, but I told him I would need it more than he did. Looks like I was right." Grady smiled victoriously.

"You mean...I shouldn't have any nightmares if I sleep here?" Ethan asked skeptically.

"If you do, I'm asking that shaman for my money back," Grady answered in mock seriousness.

"Good night, Ethan." He left the room, shutting the door behind him.

Once he was alone, aside from the dog, Ethan laid down in the bed, excited at the potential chance to have uninterrupted sleep. Out of caution, though, he placed the knife underneath his pillow.

The dog cuddled next to his legs as if to reassure him everything would be all right, and the two of them fell fast asleep.

Seven: There are No Secrets in a House with Eyes

WHEN ETHAN WOKE the next morning, his phone was buzzing in his pocket. He groggily stared at the screen with half-focused eyes. It was Arthur calling, and before Ethan could decide if he was going to answer it or not, the phone determined the fate of the call itself by going to voice mail. Ethan noticed the time. It was already noon.

He dropped the phone on the bed and smashed his face into the pillow. He'd slept through his morning classes again. That was two days he'd missed since he'd met Grady, and he was certain this was the reason for Arthur's call. It was nice to finally get a decent rest—he hardly felt bad about it. Whether it was the mystical power of the dream catcher or a welcome coincidence, Ethan hadn't dreamed a thing. The phone chimed, as if reminding him he should feel some responsibility, to let him know he had a message. He wasn't ready to be chided so he decided to save it for later.

Ethan rolled over and reached down to pet the little brown Chihuahua who had cuddled himself against his legs all night, but the dog was no longer there. He sat up to search for it and noticed the door had been cracked open. Grady or one of the ghosts must have let him out. He'd probably woken a long time ago.

He climbed out of the bed and entered the adjacent bathroom to freshen up. He was still in yesterday's clothes, as that was all he'd had with him, but he managed to get himself fresh-faced and put together. He could probably thank the long night of rest for that.

As he sat down on the bed to put on his shoes, he remembered the knife he'd foolishly stashed under the pillow. He wasn't really sure why he thought he'd needed it. A dream couldn't really hurt him, could it? It had been a late night and he clearly wanted the comfort of safety. He knew now, though, he would need to return it before Grady noticed it was missing.

He slid the knife into the hiding place in his back pocket, beneath his shirt, and slipped quietly from the room, careful not to make the door creak too much as he exited.

He followed the eerie hallway, which seemed even more so with its antiquated charm and dated decor, to the staircase. As he descended with mindful steps, he overheard voices in a state of polite conversation from the main floor. He was worried he'd be caught coming down, but once he reached the bottom, he was able to pinpoint that the voices were coming from another room farther down the hall.

Ethan slipped into the study. He rushed directly to the weapons table, pulled the knife from his pocket, and returned it to its rightful place. He let out a huge sigh of relief and turned to leave the room with the same quick and discreet pace.

"Not your style?" Grady questioned with a smirk from the doorway. Ethan's heart flopped, and he was so wildly consumed with embarrassment he thought he would spontaneously combust.

Grady awaited his response with a wry smile. His figure cut a strong silhouette as he leaned in the doorway, which only emphasized Ethan's insecurity.

The contrast between them was stark. He was the sheepish naive youth and Grady was the pinnacle of calm resolve masking inner chaos. This was highlighted by his sepia-toned golden hair, which appeared purposefully tousled, and a white long-sleeved shirt rolled to his elbows, unbuttoned at the collar but restrained by a fitted warm gray waistcoat. His matching slacks and black oxfords only helped to capitalize on Ethan's idea he was the living definition of the dashing scholar. Visually, he was precisely curated, but Ethan knew flames of torment burned beneath his bookish glazed eyes. It was a fire Ethan longed to see more of but feared being burned by.

"I...I was ..." Ethan fumbled for any words that would smooth over the indignity, but ultimately, he decided on the truth.

"I should have asked before borrowing it. Last night was... I guess the idea of having it nearby made me feel safe. I'm really sorry."

Grady glided coolly into the room.

"No need to apologize. That's precisely the reason I keep them in the first place."

"I shouldn't have taken it, though." Ethan stood firm in his apology.

Grady smiled at him. "If I hadn't wanted you to, then I would have stopped you. I knew all along, of course."

Ethan noticed a figure who was watching from the ceiling to the left of them just as the specter faded back into the house.

"Agatha," Ethan realized flatly. He should have known no secrets were held in a house that had its own eyes.

"Indeed." Grady nodded. He ran his fingers over the blade Ethan had returned and then moved to the one sitting next to it. It was roughly the same length but glinted brighter as the silver was more polished. The handle was also very plain in comparison to the ornate butt of the other.

Grady picked it up with a steady grace and handed it to Ethan.

"This one would do you better in a fight," he advised. "The other is a ceremonial dagger and rather ineffective in practical use."

"Oh…" Ethan swallowed down further embarrassment. "I didn't know."

"It's all right. You pick things up over time and with experience. I'll get you a proper sheath for that, too, so you can carry it with you."

"Oh, that's okay. I don't know that I'll actually need it," Ethan declined nervously.

"Of course, I too hope that to be the case, but I must insist you will," said Grady in a tone that let Ethan know not to argue the point. He set the knife down for the moment and clasped his hands behind his back. "But before we face the duties of the day, please, join us for brunch."

"Us?" Ethan wondered aloud, thinking of the ghosts as their only company.

"Yes, Benny is already in the dining hall. I'm afraid he couldn't wait. The boy has terrible manners." Grady sighed.

"Benny the human?" Ethan clarified.

"Oh, yes." Grady laughed. "Although, sometimes I think the dog is the one better suited for polite society."

The dining room in Grady's home was spacious but not as massive as Ethan had imagined. The dark mahogany table would comfortably seat ten but only three places were being used today. Ethan sat across from Benny, who had already finished his meal before they'd joined him and was eyeing Ethan's plate conspiratorially. Grady sat at the head of the table, reading some emails on his laptop while they ate.

"Do you usually stop by here for breakfast...err, brunch?" Ethan asked Benny, taking a bite of his eggs and remembering it was already midday.

Benny's eyebrows shot up, breaking the concentrated stare he had fixed on Ethan's bacon. He looked imploringly at Grady, as if asking permission to answer. Grady ignored them both and continued scanning whatever document had caught his interest.

Benny scratched behind his ear and then leaned forward on his elbows as if indicating he were about to divulge a great secret.

"I live here." He grinned.

"Oh," Ethan remarked with surprise. He glanced from Benny to Grady and then back again. "Oh! Are you two..."

Benny waited for him to continue as his words lingered. He raised a perplexed eyebrow and grabbed an uneaten slice of bacon from Ethan's plate and chomped it.

"Are we what?" he asked, mouth full.

"He's asking if we're a couple," Grady interjected flatly, still never letting his gaze waver from the screen. "The answer is *no*. And, Benny, we do not help ourselves to food on other people's plates."

"Sorry," Benny and Ethan said in unison, although for different reasons.

Benny cheerfully answered Ethan's question. "I needed a place to stay."

Ethan nodded and continued to eat his meal. Grady seemed rather generous with his living quarters, but Ethan didn't want to pry too much. Benny seemed to have enough bad manners for the both of them.

Grady snapped his laptop shut and rose from his seat.

"I'm heading out. I have a meeting," he announced as he gathered his belongings.

"Should I go with you?" Ethan asked eagerly. He was anxious to start whatever lessons the day entailed.

"No, I'm afraid not—it's personal business. However, Benny will be here so feel free to relax and make yourself at home. Do whatever it is you'd like. Benny usually lies about watching the Netflix until work."

"Grady, don't call it *the* Netflix." Benny shook his head with mild disgust. "It makes you sound older than you are."

"It's just as well. I *feel* older than I am," Grady retorted.

"Anyway, yeah! You can hang out with me." Benny beamed at Ethan. "I'd love to get to know you better, and then I can help you bring your stuff here."

"What?" Ethan had missed something important.

Grady rolled his eyes and sighed heavily—a mannerism Ethan guessed would become a staple of the majority of conversations that involved Benny.

"You were supposed to ease into that throughout the day," Grady scolded him.

"Oops." Benny cringed but smiled at Ethan hopefully.

"What are you guys talking about?" Ethan turned to Grady for an answer.

Grady glanced at his silver watch and ran his hand through his hair.

"I *really* must be going," Grady insisted. "So, let me save us all some time. We're going to offer that you move in temporarily. You'll decline with some feeble excuse I'll only halfway understand. I'll remind you practicality is on my side and you're not exactly safe until I've had time to train you to deal with this new lifestyle you've immersed yourself into. Then you'll give in and accept the offer with a sheepish smile as if I didn't know you wanted to accept the proposition all along. Does that sound about right? So, Benny will help you pick up your things later and you can bring them before work."

Ethan was dumbfounded at Grady's presumptuous, but not entirely inaccurate, statement. Benny continued to beam at him as if he were a child showing off a toy.

"Am I that transparent to you?" Ethan finally mumbled and ate the last bite of his meal, already guessing he knew the answer.

Grady didn't respond. He simply winked at Ethan and moved for the door. "I'll see you both this evening." He waved at them without looking back.

Benny was already out of his seat and pulling Ethan's chair away from the table.

"You're going to love it here," he exclaimed. "This place is amazing. I'll show you around!"

Ethan wasn't sure exactly how everything had happened so fast, but he had definitely learned one valuable lesson already. Grady was not accustomed to being said no to. Luckily for the doctor, there wasn't any inclination in Ethan's mind for him to ever want to say it.

Eight: The Invitation

"GRADY! SO GOOD to see you." Arthur rose from his desk to greet his friend. He glanced over the other man's shoulder and, seeing he was alone, closed the door behind them and ushered Grady to a chair by his desk.

"How are you, Arthur?" Grady asked warmly as they both seated themselves.

"Good, good," Arthur answered. "I've been trying to get a hold of Ethan, though, and he's not answering my messages. I have to admit I was starting to worry. So, it's good you're here."

"Yes, Ethan has been rather preoccupied the last couple of days," Grady said, making himself comfortable in his seat.

"So it seems. He's missed all of his classes and skipped out on having lunch with me. Not even a call or a text to let me know. You must have done a number on him because he's usually not so inconsiderate." Arthur steadied his gaze on Grady with mild disapproval.

Grady shrugged. "I bring out the worst in people." He noticed a jar of M&Ms on the desk and helped himself to a handful. This conversation was going to be unpleasant and he didn't like the idea of not having anything to do with his hands other than gesticulate. Arthur would probably do enough of that for the both of them.

"You don't mean that." Arthur wagged his finger, proving Grady's assumption correct. "Anyway, how is he?"

"He's doing rather well. He's a very enthusiastic young man, I'll give him that," Grady admitted, still trying to decide what to make of his new companion. "I think, when it comes to his personality, there's a lot of territory I still need to explore in order to understand him. He's very guarded and in an almost perpetual state of tension. It must be exhausting for him."

"Yes, that's Ethan." Arthur chuckled. "You can't blame him, though. Navigating life with only a shred of the truth of who you actually are would prove quite difficult for anyone. Have you told him yet?"

"No," Grady answered honestly. He saw the other man's face fall in concern. "I had hoped he'd guess it on his own. But he couldn't even deduce the truth about Benny and that was staring him flat in the face. He's either the most unobservant man in history or in constant denial of his basic instincts. Perhaps both."

"You have to tell him!" Arthur threw his hands up in frustration. He looked like a puffed-up owl. "That was the point of me introducing you. Then you can teach him how to deal with it all."

Grady popped a candy in his mouth and talked to the ceiling instead of directly at Arthur. "I need you to do me a favor. Rather, two favors."

"Anything. What is it?" Arthur agreed instantaneously as his ruffled feathers settled.

"You have to cease contact with Ethan." Before his words had time to sink in, he popped another candy in his mouth. "Also, he mentioned you and his mother are close. I need you to keep her preoccupied. It would be best not to have any prying phone calls or visits to my house while he's living there."

"He's already living with you?" Arthur was shocked. "You do work fast."

"Will you see to it, please?" Grady stared at Arthur both piercingly and pleadingly.

"Well, if I'm a distraction to the success of your therapy, then of course I won't mind stepping aside." Arthur sighed. "However, I can't control Karen. She's used to seeing her son every weekend, so she'll start asking questions soon."

"Then give her something else to think about," Grady suggested. "Ethan said you had a crush on her. Ask her on a date this weekend."

"Don't be absurd!" Arthur was flustered and clearly beside himself; a state in which Grady had never seen the man in all their years of friendship. "Ethan said that, really? No. No, that won't work."

"Why not?" Grady shrugged as if it were clearly the best solution.

"Well, if my affection is so obvious to Ethan, then I'm afraid it would be as obvious to his mother, and in the twenty years of friendship we've had, she has never indicated she felt likewise. I may *be* a fool, but I will not *make* a fool of myself."

"Unrequited love. How romantic of you, Arthur." Grady smirked, finishing off the last M&M.

"Hardly." Arthur rolled his eyes. "Besides, I would never be good enough for her. Look at me! She's practically a goddess in comparison and ten years younger. Beautiful, smart, kind, and surprisingly optimistic. *You* should meet her! She would charm you right off your feet."

"I quite like my feet planted firmly on the ground, thank you. Besides, the last thing I need is an overprotective mother tagging along and sticking her nose in my business." Without the candy to save him, Grady found himself wagging his index finger at Arthur now. "Which is precisely why you must keep her distracted. I don't really care how you do it. I don't need any outside persuasion meddling with Ethan at the present moment."

Arthur stared at Grady in momentary silence, and then signs of worry emerged in the lines of his face. "I don't care for your tone, Grady. I'm starting to find your request a bit unsettling."

"Do you trust me?" Grady asked pointedly.

"I always have... You promised me when he was old enough that you would help him. You are going to teach him to suppress his powers? Like you do with everyone else?"

"That is my modus operandi, is it not?" Grady countered, sensing the tension in the room rising.

"Then why haven't you told him yet?" Arthur pressed. "You haven't told him anything, and yet you've somehow convinced him to give up his friends and family and move in with you. That's not exactly normal."

"I haven't asked him to give up anything."

"So you're asking it of me, behind his back? That's even more alarming."

Grady sensed his friend's loyalty on the matter slipping away.

"Will you help me or not?" Grady asked with an air of finality.

"First, I must ask *you* something." Arthur crossed his arms and stared somberly into Grady's eyes. "I should have asked it a long time ago and now I'm wondering if it's too late... When you contacted me several years ago, you had just moved here. There were no records of you or your past. No one knew anything about you, yet you seemed to know everything about everyone else. You sent me an invitation to a party, telling me I was your favorite author."

"Is this flashback sequence of yours going anywhere?" Grady huffed, glancing at his watch even though he didn't have anywhere else to be.

"We became great friends," Arthur continued, ignoring the interruption. "However, there is *one* detail that has been troubling me. A few years ago, I was in your study, perusing your bookshelf, and I found *one* of my books. It struck me as odd because if I were your *favorite* author as you'd insisted, then the other dozen books I've written should have been there too. You know which book I speak of."

Grady shifted uncomfortably in his seat. It was true. Grady knew exactly what book it was and why the other man would now, more than ever, be so concerned. Arthur pulled a copy of it out of his top desk drawer and let it fall with a heavy thump onto the desk between them.

Arthur read the title aloud. "*The Mechanics of Sleep Travel.*"

Grady sat in guilty silence, trying to conjure whatever story he'd fabricated long ago for this very moment.

"It's a genius work. Why wouldn't I showcase it in my collection?" he finally answered with an absentminded shrug.

"I didn't write this book and I think you know that," Arthur chided. Grady dropped his gaze to the book because at this moment it was easier to acknowledge it than his friend's accusing glare.

"It was published in my name to give it more credence so it stood a chance of reaching more people. Of course my critics panned it and everyone decided I had finally gone off the deep end, but I didn't care about my sinking reputation. Its real author, Vincent Roam, needed it to exist, in the hopes it would speak to someone out there and bring them to him. So, he and I waited for a response, and after a couple of years, he passed away without anyone showing the slightest bit of interest. I was the one left waiting and I had given up. Until one day, you arrived in town and sought me out. In the twenty-two years since it's been published, you are the only person who has ever shown genuine interest in it. And yet, you do not possess the ability to travel to other worlds in your sleep. But here you are now, in my office, telling me I'm to no longer have contact with the one person who *can* and that he's essentially become your prisoner. And he doesn't even realize it yet."

"I don't like when you're melodramatic, Arthur. It makes you sound like my father."

"I said I had a question for you and I want the honest answer," Arthur demanded. "Are you really here to help Ethan?"

"Of course I am," Grady spat. "Of course that's my intention."

"I trust that it's your intention, but is it your *priority*?" Arthur countered emphatically. "I know you, Grady, probably better than anyone else on the planet, and even then that's not saying a lot. You always have good intentions. The problem that I've been losing sleep over lately is—are yours the kind of good intentions that pave the road to Hell, as they say? I've seen it firsthand. You take over someone's life, their emotions and their senses, with a whirlwind of charm and mystique. But, let's face it. You have a bad habit of leaving trails of death and destruction in your wake."

The weight of these words were not lost on Grady, and although he knew Arthur was referencing the people and creatures they had known in their time together, the only face that entered Grady's mind was the woman he had lost those many years ago, the moment this life had all started. A lifetime of defeat and torment must have shown on his face as Arthur instantaneously produced regret.

"I'm sorry, Grady," he said softly. "I wasn't talking about that, and you know I wasn't."

"I know," Grady whispered flatly. He took a moment to gather himself and finally responded to his friend's concerns.

"You're perfectly right, though." He wiped the sweat from his palms onto the knees of his slacks. "You would be remiss not to question my judgment with Ethan, but I assure you, he will be safe with me."

"Good. Because I promised his father I would spend the rest of my days protecting his family, so if anything happens to Ethan, you can bet your life you will have me to answer to," Arthur said, deadly serious.

"Then it's a good thing nothing will happen to him," Grady answered simply but did not meet his gaze.

"I hope you're right." Arthur sighed. "I would never be able to live with myself if I had handed the most precious soul in the world over to the one man his father would have despised."

"After all these years, do you really think so little of me?" Grady wasn't really offended, at least not entirely. He knew perfectly well Arthur was a good man and concerned about all the right things. He could never hold that against him.

"No. Of course not," Arthur answered kindly. "I have a bad feeling. Maybe if I say my fears out loud, then they won't come to pass."

"What a silly superstitious belief. You give too much of yourself away, Arthur." Grady rose from his seat decidedly. He didn't see any reason to continue the conversation at this point.

"I suppose I always have," Arthur agreed.

"Anyway, as much as I enjoyed the trip down memory lane and the altruistic threats, you'll be comforted to know you won't be parted from your precious Ethan too long," Grady replied. "I have come to invite you to my annual Halloween party."

He slipped an invitation out of his jacket pocket and let it fall on top of the book Arthur had finished confronting him with.

"I hope to see you there, Arthur. Maybe then you'll see everything is as it should be." And with that, Grady left him sitting alone in his office.

Nine: Benny's Curse

"EVERY YEAR GRADY hosts this huge Halloween party here for all of his clients," Benny was explaining as he and Ethan brought the last box of Ethan's belongings to his room.

Earlier in the afternoon, they had borrowed an old pickup truck Grady had on his property and went to Ethan's apartment to pack his things. He didn't actually own much so it only took a couple of hours to load it all. He went ahead and put in his notice, too, since he wasn't sure how long he'd be gone. He figured there wasn't any point in paying rent for an apartment he wouldn't even be living in.

Though it was actually his mother who paid his rent. He knew he'd need to call her sometime to let her know he'd moved. He wasn't sure exactly what he was going to say to her yet. How does one explain moving in with their boss after only knowing them for a couple of days? He had enough going on, so he decided to put that conversation on hold for now.

"Really?" Ethan sat the last box down. He sat down on the floor and unpacked a few things. Benny followed his lead and did the same.

"I would think supernatural creatures would be pretty busy on Halloween," Ethan reasoned. "Why would they want to waste it going to a human's silly party?"

"Oh, it's not silly at all!" Benny shook his head as if Ethan were entirely misguided. "And definitely not a waste.

Grady spares no expense! It's like one of those fancy masquerades you see in movies. Everyone who is anyone in the supernatural community will be there. It's the social event of the year."

"Sounds impressive," Ethan said genuinely. He had unpacked most of his clothes and set them out on the bed in an effort to decide what he should wear later. He'd still not managed to ask what the dress code was for this kind of job. Professional? Casual? Easy-to-dodge-monsters-in?

"How did Grady gain such clout, though?" Ethan wondered. "I mean, he's human after all. Is he that good at everything he does?"

"He is." Benny nodded. "And they're scared of him."

Ethan laughed.

"Why is that funny?" Benny took some books out of a box and flipped through them before stacking them off to the side.

"A bunch of monsters scared of a man. I mean, really, they're his clients first of all. Why would he harm them? What's the worst he could possibly do?"

"Kill them," Benny answered matter-of-factly, pulling out some picture frames and considering the photos.

"Are you serious?"

"He's done it before. Lots of times… That's how this all works," Benny explained. "If a supernatural brings attention to themselves by killing, haunting, possessing, et cetera, then Grady hunts them down and gives them an ultimatum. He offers them the chance to reform their ways, and if they don't agree, then he exterminates them."

"Wow." Ethan was genuinely surprised. "How does he manage that? I mean, aren't they more powerful than him?"

"More powerful than most people. But Grady isn't most people. He's devoted his entire life to this. Sure, he can be the most generous person you've ever met if you're on his good side, but if you're on his bad side..."

Benny shuddered. "He goes dead inside. It's like he completely blacks out with cold, calculating rage. Once he goes there...well...you don't want to be the target. At least that's the gossip. I haven't seen him do it yet, but I've heard a lot of ghosts say they've never met anyone like him. And the vampires are fascinated by him. I think they play along with his ultimatums just for the chance to spend more time with him."

"I don't know about that. Maybe he's good at playing the part," Ethan responded carefully. He wasn't sure how many people knew Grady's past or if it was something he'd only shared with Ethan. He didn't want to divulge any secrets, but he was oddly protective over his new friend. *Benny's wrong. Grady couldn't possibly be that horrible. Could he?* "Maybe... He's only ever been good to me."

Benny smiled optimistically.

"Anyway, Halloween usually *is* when they like to cause the most trouble. That's why Grady started the parties. It's an easy way to keep tabs on everyone, and they still get the benefit of being mischievous but in Grady's house and under his watchful eye. It keeps them away from the temptation outside these walls to mess with any other humans. Plus, I think they really like the music and the chance for good gossip."

"Do we get to go to the party? I mean, we're not his *clients* and we're not supernatural."

Benny stared at him with an expression of sheer amusement. "Are we not?"

"What's that supposed to mean?"

Benny rolled his eyes. "I mean there's your life *before* you met Grady and then your life *after* you met Grady. You're never really normal after that."

Ethan mulled the statement over for a minute and then shrugged. "How did you meet Grady, anyway?"

"We ran into each other in the cemetery— Aww, you used to have a puppy!" Benny grinned, holding a frame that contained a photo of a twelve-year-old Ethan and a German shepherd.

"Yeah...You were saying," Ethan pressed.

"I knew you were a dog person." Benny set the photo down with a pleased grin. "Before I met Grady, I lived with an old lady."

"Your mom?"

Benny shook his head.

"Your grandmother?"

Benny shook his head again. "No, just an old lady. *Anyway*, I would eat breakfast, run around outside, sleep, eat lunch, run around outside, sleep, eat dinner..."

"Did you not go to school or have a job?" Ethan interjected.

Benny laughed and continued his story without addressing Ethan's question. "In the evenings, though, I would sneak out and run through the cemetery nearby because on the other side is an Italian restaurant. I had befriended the guy who owned it. He would always give me free food."

"You sure seemed to eat a lot... I guess that hasn't changed since you met Grady," Ethan teased, recalling his swiped bacon that morning.

Benny scoffed. "Rude! Also, you interrupt too much."

"Sorry," Ethan said, leaning against the bed as he motioned for Benny to continue.

"One night, I was on my way through the cemetery and I saw Grady and this woman arguing. It was Marguerite. They were strangers to me then, and I thought it was weird to see people fighting in the cemetery in the middle of the night so I went to investigate. I don't know what she said to him, but he grabbed her by the arm pretty forcefully and she started struggling. I ran to try to break it up. Unfortunately for me, but I guess fortunately for Grady, I stepped right in the line of fire. She had cast a curse at him at the exact moment I wedged between them. The shock of what had happened gave her a chance to escape, and she took off before Grady could do anything. He brought me home that night and has taken care of me ever since."

"I'm so sorry. That's terrible. What kind of curse was it?"

"This." Benny waved a hand at his own form. "You still can't guess? C'mon, Ethan! Who has been missing from the house all day?"

It only took a moment and reality finally hit Ethan like a harsh awakening. He heard Grady's words echo in his mind. *Technically, the dog came first.*

"You're a dog!" Ethan exclaimed, pointing at him.

"No, I *was* a dog. Now I'm a human. Part of the time, anyway. Vivian likes to call me a Reverse Werehuahua. She thinks it's funny. Grady insists it's entirely different than being a werewolf, though. He'd never have me if I were a werewolf." He seemed relieved now his secret was out.

"You're a dog," Ethan repeated.

Benny laughed.

"Yes. At night, I'm a dog, and during the day, I'm human. Grady thinks Marguerite was trying to turn him into a werewolf since he hates them so much; but since the curse hit me instead, it had unexpected effects. He's been trying to convince her to fix me ever since, but she refuses just to spite him."

Ethan was still processing everything and wondering how he could have not noticed the entire time.

"You slept curled at my legs last night!"

"Well, yes, Ethan," Benny retorted. "When I'm a dog, I'm a *dog*. I can't fight my instincts. I do normal dog stuff. Besides, I left the room as soon as I turned into a human."

"You weren't wearing any clothes as a dog," Ethan pointed out.

"I left the room as soon as I turned into a nude human."

Ethan grabbed a nearby pillow and threw it at Benny. Benny caught it before it hit him in the face. He was good at playing catch, after all.

"I can't believe you!" He was surprised by Benny's lack of decorum.

"Oh, please, Ethan! Don't pretend it bothers you. I've seen the way you look at Grady. Have you ever even had a girlfriend before?"

"Don't change the subject," Ethan warned, his cheeks flush. "This conversation was about you, not me."

They stared at each other for a moment as if deciding where to go from here, now that both of their secrets were out. Suddenly, they burst into a fit of laughter. Perhaps it was to break the tension or because they now shared an inside joke. Whatever the reason, he and Benny now understood each other so much better than hours before.

After a minute or so of nonstop laughing, the bedroom door swung open and Grady stepped inside. He glanced down at them quizzically as they recovered from their fit.

"What is going on in here? You're being awfully loud."

"Sorry, Grady," Benny said, still giggling. "We didn't know you were here."

"I don't see what my whereabouts have to do with your sound levels, but yes, I dropped in for a moment to get something. What is it? What's so funny?"

"It's nothing," Benny answered. "But here's some good news. Ethan finally realized I'm a dog!"

"It was kind of obvious," Ethan admitted, barely believing that it'd been so hard for him to put two and two together earlier.

"Painfully obvious, I should say," Grady said. "Good for you, then. That leaves one less thing for me to have to explain today. Although, I'm sure a hundred more questions will rise in its place. So, if you two can manage to pull yourselves together, then please get ready for work. Dacey is coming in tonight and you know how he feels about punctuality. It's a virtue everyone except for him should possess as it's the only way to guarantee him a fashionably late entrance."

The remark reminded Ethan of the question he kept forgetting to ask. "What should I wear? I don't really know how an apprentice should dress."

"Ethan, if you were to die tonight, how would you want to be remembered? Wear that." Grady gestured to his own fashionable attire, obviously well aware of how handsome he was, and with a self-satisfied smirk, he exited the room.

It then occurred to Ethan even a minute detail, like clothing, was a meticulously planned move on Grady's part. *Is there anything he does that isn't premeditated?*

BENNY HAD LEFT Ethan alone to get changed.

Grady had advised wearing something that reflected how he'd want to be remembered if he died. He had eventually settled on wearing a plain black T-shirt, blue jeans, and black Converse sneakers. It was simple and forgettable, which was how he viewed himself. It might not impress Grady, but it was the role he was comfortable in.

He sat down on his bed and took in the room that would now be his sanctuary for however long he needed. It was strange, but he actually felt more at home here than he ever had in his apartment. Perhaps it was the warmth of the decor. The autumnal colors of crimson and amber dominated the space, and a peaceful painting of a dreamy woodland landscape drew attention as the focal point of the room. Or maybe he felt at home because of the comfort of the dream catcher placed above his headboard, assuring a good night's sleep.

Ethan pulled his phone out of his pocket and scanned through his missed messages from earlier in the day. Now that he had a moment to himself, he decided he'd better call Arthur. He'd realized too late he'd skipped out on lunch with him and was now guilt ridden.

He placed the call, but the phone only rang a few times and went to voice mail.

"Hey, Arthur. It's Ethan. Sorry I missed lunch...and class...again. I've been really busy, but I wanted to let you know everything is going fine. Thanks for introducing me to Grady. I think he might actually be able to help me with my sleeping problems. Anyway, I'll talk to you later. Bye."

He pressed End and headed out.

GRADY LOCKED THE doors to the study behind him. He didn't have much time to himself and he needed to hurry.

He walked swiftly to the large cherrywood bookcase and quickly scanned the titles until he found what he was searching for:

The Mechanics of Sleep Travel by Dr. Arthur Ellis.

It had been a careless mistake to leave the tome with the rest of his collection. He should have realized the first place any author would inspect in a friend's home would be their bookshelf. It was a mistake that could cost him everything he'd been working toward.

He pulled the book out and stared at the cover as if it had betrayed him in some way. Which of course was silly. He had betrayed himself. There was no question now Grady knew of Ethan's existence before he ever met him. That it was his entire reason for moving to such a tedious place as Shady Pines. Every town had its own ghosts, demons, and choice of monsters. Shady Pines wasn't special in the least. Except that it held one creature that didn't exist anywhere else in the world. And he had been stupid enough to leave a trail of evidence that he was aware of it.

Of course he would have to tell Ethan what he was and it would have to be soon. However, he didn't have to tell him everything. Only enough to soothe his curiosity and then he would shield him from the rest. Ethan could never know the whole truth. It would jeopardize the careful balancing act Grady had been keeping in motion.

This book was his map to finding Ethan, but now it only served as a weapon in the wrong hands. In Grady's opinion, that was everyone's hands, especially Ethan's.

He walked to the fireplace, which was crackling with heat and spitting flame as if warning him not to carry on with his insane paranoia. Watchful eyes were upon him.

"Leave. I wish to be alone!" Grady's voice was firm and unwavering as he spoke to the air around him. An elongated shadow, which had crept along the walls, now disappeared back inside them, and he knew that he was truly alone now.

He paused, running his hand along the cover as if saying goodbye to an old friend. He knew what he must do but was torn inside. He tossed the book into the fire, even though it made him feel like a villain to do so.

A void opened in his chest, but his breath stayed steady as the flames licked away the truth from the pages.

This act had calmed him. For even if he were not a villain, he was most certainly not a hero.

It was the role *he* was comfortable in.

Ten: Ravishing & Ravaging

THE THREE MEN arrived at Grady's office together promptly. Vivian had already beaten them there, and a scowl crossed Grady's face as they opened the door.

A tall and muscular man was leaning on the counter, nose to nose with Vivian. His messy black hair fell into his blue eyes as he whispered something to her, causing her to giggle with delight. They both turned their attention to the front as Grady, Ben, and Ethan walked in.

"Let's at least *pretend* this is a professional office," Grady rebuked. "Public displays of affection aren't allowed on the clock."

"Oh, but when *you* do it, it's okay?" the man countered, turning to face them.

"Of course. It's my office. I can do whatever I like." Grady took off his coat and hung it on a nearby brass rack.

"Well, Vivian is my girlfriend, so I can do whatever *I* like."

Vivian cleared her throat.

"Well, whatever she'll let me do, anyway," he corrected with a grin. His smile filled his stubbled and chiseled face nearly as largely as his thick eyebrows.

"She may be your girlfriend, but when she's at work, she's my secretary, so please, break it up."

"Fine, fine." He leaned over the counter and gave Vivian a kiss. "See ya later, babe."

"Bye, Thomas." She smiled wistfully after him.

"Bye, Thomas," Benny echoed. He seemed over the moon to see Vivian's boyfriend.

Thomas nodded a greeting of acknowledgement toward Ethan and patted Benny on his head on the way out.

"That was Thomas," Benny happily informed Ethan.

"So I heard." Ethan smirked.

Benny beamed. "He's awesome. He always smells like barbecue and sandalwood. When I'm in dog form, he lets me lick his face."

"You should try it in human form sometime and see if he's still as *awesome* about it," Grady teased.

"You think so?" Benny asked, not picking up on the sarcasm.

Ethan pursed his lips and shook his head to let him know not to really do it. Benny looked defeated.

"I don't know why you like him. He's quite insufferable," Grady remarked disapprovingly as he walked past Vivian toward his office.

"He's no such thing!" She laughed. "He's handsome and charming. And that's exactly why you hate him."

"I don't hate him," Grady said, leaning on the doorframe. "I wouldn't mind if he was ravaged by a vengeful horned demon or two, but that doesn't mean that I *hate* him."

He grinned at her. She rolled her eyes but returned his grin.

"I must say the only horny demon doing any ravaging here will be me." A precocious voice cut through the room.

Standing at the entrance was another raven-haired man. This one appeared a bit younger, though, roughly in his mid-twenties. He was very pale with piercing green eyes. He was slightly taller than Ethan but a tad shy of meeting Grady in height. His frame was slender, and he sauntered toward them with all the confidence and swagger of someone who had spent too many years hearing adoration thrust upon them.

He wore tight-fitting black pants, a black V-neck T-shirt with a crimson damask waistcoat, various pieces of gothic jewelry on his wrists and fingers, and black boots with entirely too many buckles for any sensible man. He looked like a rock star, and Ethan couldn't take his eyes off him.

Grady seemed to notice Ethan's fixation and let out an annoyed grunt. However, he quickly plastered on his signature charming grin and moved to meet the man.

Ethan was certain Benny growled.

"Ten minutes late. So you're right on time," Grady remarked as they wrapped their arms around one another in a welcoming embrace.

"Only ten?" The man pouted, but his green eyes danced with merriment. "I shall have to try better to be otherwise engaged next time. I was shooting for fifteen at the very least."

"Or you could have not come in at all. That'd been fine too," Benny muttered. Grady shot him a glance of reproach. He rolled his eyes and walked out of the lobby and down the hallway, disappearing from the group.

"Forgive Benny. He's a little—" Grady started.

"*Ruff* around the edges?" The man said and then laughed at his own terrible pun. His gaze was then caught by Ethan, who had been silently gawking at him since he'd walked through the door.

"Who is this doe-eyed poppet?" he asked, resting hungry eyes upon Ethan.

"Dacey, this is my apprentice, Ethan. Ethan, this is Dacey. He's a client and a vampire."

Dacey slapped Grady upside the arm and scoffed openly.

"Really? Just a client, huh? Is that what you're telling yourself these days?" Dacey smirked.

Grady shot him a reproachful look. "Don't," he said quietly—almost too quietly for Ethan to hear.

"Fine, my ambiguous Narcissus." Dacey gave in with a bored sigh, brushing a few loose locks of hair out of his face. "Then let's go play doctor, shall we?" He winked at Ethan.

Grady gestured for Dacey to take the lead, which he did, locking his arm through Ethan's, as they walked into the office.

"Apprentice, you say? I'm certainly in for trouble if there's two of you I have to entertain now," Dacey remarked, sounding far too pleased with this new development.

Grady gave Vivian an imploring look, but she just shook her head, her lips curled in amusement.

Dacey unlinked his arm from Ethan's and wandered to the black and gold-gilded Victorian sectional sofa Grady supplied for his clients. He made himself right at home as if he'd sat there a hundred times before and crossed his left leg over the other, grabbed the toe of his boot with his right hand, and lifted his left index finger to rest thoughtfully atop his pale strawberry-tinted lips as he examined Grady's new apprentice.

Ethan and Grady took their seats in a couple of armchairs, which sat across from him, and Grady reviewed his file and scribbled the date and time on a notepad. Ethan said the name on the file aloud as he glanced over it.

"Dacey Sinnett."

"Emphasis on *Sin*." Dacey winked at him.

Ethan's cheeks flushed and it became hard to maintain eye contact. Then he had a curious thought and decided to chance an inquiry.

"I hope I'm not being rude in asking this, but if you're a vampire, how are you out before the sun sets? I thought you couldn't be in direct sunlight. Or is that a myth?"

"It's not rude at all. I'm rather the braggart on answering that question." Dacey grinned widely. "Everyone is quite jealous of my superior standing in this town, you see. It was a gift bestowed upon me at Grady's goodwill by that little enchantress of his that captains the lobby."

"Vivian put a spell on you?"

"Mmm," Dacey affirmed. "As long as I stay on her good side, I'm free to dance in the face of my weakness. The sun destroys others of my kind but only bestows glorious sensuous kisses upon *my* cheek." He demonstrated by lightly caressing his face as if he were an actor on stage for a captive audience.

Ethan was impressed by Vivian's skill but also perplexed by Grady's motivation to allow it. Hadn't Benny told him Grady tried to stop people from utilizing their *talents*?

As if he knew what Ethan was thinking, Grady interjected, "The sun is only a temporary fan of yours, Dacey. So long as your daytime activities remain of use to me."

Dacey nodded. "I'm quite aware of the fleeting nature of all good things, but I do so enjoy delighting in them while I can."

"Let's get to it, shall we?" Grady cleared his throat. "We'll start with some of the usual questions."

"Really? Is that necessary?" Dacey interrupted in a blasé tone. "Your dutiful checklist is so dull. Besides, I want to get to know my new friend Ethan better."

"Ethan is here to observe. He's not your friend and you needn't know more about him."

"It's my business to know everyone," Dacey countered and smiled graciously at Ethan. "Especially the fine young men of this town. Tell me, Ethan, what's your name in its entirety? Is it real or make-believe like our good doctor's?"

"Ethan Jasper Roam. It's my real name." Ethan swore he saw a kindling of new interest in the vampire's eyes.

"Roam," Dacey repeated adoringly. "I like it. It's a strong name and an honest name as it's truly your own. Come, Ethan Jasper Roam, and sit next to me."

Something about Dacey's personality and self-confidence was so entirely compelling Ethan didn't even hesitate. It was as if his body had decided its motions before his reason, and he found himself walking to the alluring vampire and taking a seat beside him.

Grady fell uncharacteristically silent as he watched them. Dacey positioned himself sideways on the seat in order to lock eyes with Ethan, a flirtatious smile delicately danced across his cherub-like lips.

"Names are a very small part of us, you know," Dacey said to Ethan. "They tell others where we come from. Sometimes, they guide us to follow the paths of our fathers. Other than that, they mean little. One can *make* a name for himself, and that is something else entirely. Grady has done that. I've done that. I think you will do that too. However, a name is simply a label. Like that on a patient's chart." He nodded toward Grady's papers.

"It is so very rare that we get to glimpse anything honest or real from those that we meet. Any essence of who they really are is not going to be found in their name. It's buried underneath whatever mask they choose to wear." Dacey made his point by reaching to brush his thumb gently across Ethan's cheekbone, which caused Ethan to blush. The reaction seemed to please the vampire.

"I've found people reveal nothing of their true selves except within their art and their sin," he added. At this point, he ventured a soft but accusing glance in Grady's direction. It was fleeting, though, as his attention was quickly back on Ethan.

Dacey leaned in slightly closer. If he were human, Ethan would have been able to feel his breath upon him. Instead, the sensation was olfactory. He was immersed in a mild but effective scent of jasmine and spice. The vampire's intense gaze seared his soul with a sense of yearning and significance.

"You can find honesty in one's eyes, though. You have the stars in *your* eyes, Ethan Roam," Dacey whispered. "And worlds behind them."

Grady cleared his throat, breaking the spell.

Dacey finally tore his attention away from Ethan. He let out a chortle and bit his bottom lip.

"Don't be jealous, Grady," Dacey teased. "I feel as if I've known Ethan for a long time...or perhaps, it was just in a dream I once had."

"Don't listen to a word he's said, Ethan," Grady growled. "He's toying with you."

Dacey chuckled. "That's rich. Coming from the master puppeteer himself."

"Can we please get this appointment over with?" Grady sighed and rubbed his temples. Ethan was dazed as he stared back and forth between the two.

Dacey pouted. "You're so tedious today, Grady, what's wrong with you?"

"I have a lot on my plate at the moment and really no time for these games of yours."

"I'm afraid it's my fault," Ethan interjected helpfully. "I'm probably a huge distraction. I ask too many questions and know very little about...well...anything it seems. All of this...*stuff*...is new to me."

"A clean slate," Dacey said jubilantly. "A canvas waiting to be colored with all the pleasures and trepidation of existence. I must say, I'm quite happy to have met you, Ethan."

"And I've a feeling I'll be quite sorry I introduced the two of you," Grady murmured. "Now, please." He waved the notepad at the two of them.

"Oh, yes, your beloved procedural questions, Doctor," Dacey said, giving Grady his full attention at last. "I have them memorized as you've asked me a dozen times before. Have I had any violent encounters with any other preternaturals recently? No. Have I bestowed the gift of the vam*pyre* upon anyone? No. Have I imbibed human blood? Should I answer that one? You already know. And finally, my favorite question of all—"

"We can skip the last question, Dacey. Thank you," Grady interrupted. Ethan frowned—was there something that Grady didn't want him to hear?

"Have I recently fornicated with any humans, thus causing turmoil in their daily lives..." Dacey continued, ignoring the request to stop. "Yes. As to the latter part of the question, you would know better than I would the answer to that. Although, I might venture to say *yes*, seeing as you've been in quite an ill-mannered state this evening."

"Was that necessary?" Grady admonished him.

"What? I was being honest and answering your silly questionnaire. Was that not what you wanted?" Dacey fumbled with a string on his waistcoat, feigning innocence.

"He's supposed to learn from you, correct? Then let him learn from your mistakes as well as your accomplishments. You'd do him many favors if you were gracious enough to impart that kind of knowledge."

The silence that fell over the room felt thick enough to suffocate Ethan.

Grady sighed. "You're garishly childish." He rose and walked over to a small rolling bar near his desk and poured the contents of a bottle into a glass. He topped it with an ornately perforated spoon, a cube of sugar, and set it under a drip. Ethan noted the drink had the same green tint as Dacey's eyes.

Dacey chortled. "Ah, yes, absinthe. Makes the heart grow fonder, they say. I do miss being able to enjoy it. That bitter but relaxing taste of licorice will haunt me forever. I have only romanticized memories to tide me. Do you drink, Ethan?"

"No," Ethan answered simply. He wasn't really sure where he stood in this conversation anymore.

"A blank canvas and virtuous too? You're lucky to have found this one, Grady. Please, try not to ruin him. I'd love to have that luxury to myself."

Grady took a sip of his drink as if it could somehow calm the silent rage they could all see rising to the surface.

"I'm afraid I've ruined the mood of the evening for our doctor," Dacey said, his tone more conciliatory. "I shudder to think I might have lost myself an invitation to the biggest party of the year. I would be dreadfully inconsolable if this were the case."

Grady smiled. "Of course you're invited, Dacey. I can't imagine what my parties would be like without you. You make yourself the pièce de résistance."

"They would be entirely drab without me," Dacey agreed. "And what of young Ethan here? Will he be in attendance?"

Ethan glanced hopefully at Grady since he hadn't been formally offered the opportunity.

"Of course he'll be there," Grady said. "He lives with me."

Ethan was victorious. Dacey's expression turned to one of pure astonishment, and then he burst into an incongruous amount of laughter at the revelation.

"Well, that explains everything then, doesn't it? My apologies, Grady. I had no idea I was causing such a large dose of domestic drama for you. I'm rather beside myself now."

"Well, pull yourself together. It's not what you think."

"You're amassing a household of gorgeous men, and I dare say I feel rather jealous I've not also been extended the privilege of moving in," Dacey quipped, rising from the couch. Ethan followed his lead and also stood.

"I think we both know I couldn't handle you being around that often."

Dacey smiled coquettishly at Ethan. "It's true. I am a *handful*. Grady knows all about *that*."

Grady choked on the last sip of his drink.

"Well, I'd better be off," Dacey said. "The night is young and so are the men who I'm meeting. As always, it's been entirely my pleasure to see you, Grady. I do hope you'll forgive all of my transgressions this evening."

Grady mumbled without really answering.

Dacey smirked and turned to face Ethan.

"May I borrow your phone?"

Unsure why a vampire would want his cell phone, Ethan pulled it out of his pocket and offered it to him. Dacey took it, typed in his number, and then handed it over with a bold grin.

"If you find the doctor unqualified in whatever *areas* of interest you may have in this new life of yours, Ethan, do give me a call. I would thoroughly enjoy getting to know you more *intimately.*" Dacey winked. "You have something of a destiny in those doe eyes of yours. I'd like to see you develop. I've watched Grady's progression over the years, and it has been truly fascinating."

"Um, thanks," Ethan said, slipping his phone back into his pocket. His heart was racing, and he was certain the vampire could sense it.

"I don't think I'll ever be as impressive as Grady, though."

"I suppose you're right," Dacey said, smiling adoringly at Grady. Then he leaned in and whispered with a resolute kindness into Ethan's ear. "I think you'll be better."

With that, he bid them both adieu.

So much had changed within that short sitting. All of the wonderful and horrible things Dacey had made him feel and think... How much of it was his own genuine curiosity and how much was the influence of the vampire's poeticism? It was difficult to distinguish, but it left him deeply affected all the same, and the thrill was intoxicating.

Eleven: Lessons

"YOU'RE GOING TO get yourself killed like that," Grady said as he shut the door to his office behind the vampire. He glanced at Ethan with annoyance as he rounded his way to his desk.

"Like what?" Ethan asked in bewilderment. "With awkward conversations?"

"With your easily enamored nature." With indignation, he sat and added, "The fascination, the flirtation, the incessant blushing. Really, can you not control yourself? You do it too often. You were like putty in his hands. With a vampire, that kind of behavior is completely reckless."

At first, Ethan was insulted, but then something else occurred to him.

"You were jealous." He smiled wittingly.

"Don't be ridiculous," Grady retorted. "And you would be wise to erase that number from your phone."

"I don't know," Ethan said coyly. "Not everyone can say they can contact a vampire at the press of a button. Well, I guess you can. You two are obviously—"

Grady cut him off. "Nothing is ever obvious about me, in case you haven't worked that out yet. You'd also do well to quit guessing at my relationship status as I have none. Nor do I want one."

Ethan decided to placate the man, but he had no intention of deleting the number.

"I'll never call it," he swore.

Grady rubbed his temples. "Please, don't. He'd be so pleased with himself we'd never hear the end of it."

"Would he really kill me?"

"He said you have the stars in your eyes, Ethan." Grady smirked. "No, Dacey wouldn't have killed you. At least not anytime soon. He was completely smitten by you."

"Really?" Ethan couldn't keep the optimism out of his voice.

Grady tossed his notepad into his top right drawer and closed it a little too forcefully. "Don't feel too flattered. Catching the eye of a monster isn't exactly something to be excited about."

"He doesn't seem all that bad," Ethan argued. "He was—"

"Arrogant, narcissistic, churlish—" Grady started whirling adjectives out like they were shuriken.

"Cool," Ethan said dreamily.

"You thought he was *cool*?" Grady affected a pout. "I suppose I should start wearing tighter pants."

Ethan snorted.

"It's hard not to find everything fascinating," he finally admitted.

"I suppose that's inevitable. The feeling will go away in time." Grady smiled softly in an assuring manner.

"I don't blush *that* much, do I?" Ethan asked, crinkling his nose with embarrassment.

Grady chuckled. "You're practically a kewpie doll."

Ethan groaned with disdain at himself.

"Don't worry. That goes away with experience. You have to learn to control your emotions. At least outwardly."

"Always so much to learn," Ethan bemoaned.

"Life is a never-ending lesson," Grady agreed. "Speaking of, I have something for you. Give me a moment."

Grady left the office. Ethan sat on the edge of his desk and replayed the scene that had transpired between himself and Dacey. He was completely flustered by the entire ordeal. There were so many questions he wished he could ask Grady but didn't dare to. It would be entirely inappropriate, and he most likely wouldn't get any direct answers anyway.

Grady returned holding a black leather jacket and a matching belt with a sheath. He handed it over, and Ethan accepted it dutifully.

"These are yours now." Grady rested his hands on his hips and watched Ethan with a sentimental expression. "The knife I'd promised. I haven't worn the jacket in nearly a decade so it's a tad out of fashion and probably a bit too large, I'm afraid, but it's what's inside that counts."

Ethan set the sheathed knife and belt down on the desk and unfolded the jacket to reveal it was lined with hidden pockets.

Grady pointed things out with pride. "You'll have to memorize all the locations, but you've got pockets of holy water, frankincense, bits of silver, rosemary, bloodstone, et cetera. All of the essentials."

Ethan noticed an empty strap that lined part of the left front of the jacket. "What's that for?"

"Oh yes!" Grady walked around the desk and opened a drawer. "I've got wood for you."

Ethan whipped his head up. "What?"

Grady held a sharpened piece of ash wood and grinned wickedly. "Stakes."

Ethan smiled and took the stake from Grady, placing it into the strap.

"They're hard and pointy and they get the job done." Grady winked.

Ethan rolled his eyes.

"You didn't blush that time. You're already improving."

Ethan laughed. "Okay, but please stop talking like a that's-what-she-said joke. It's really distracting." He slid the jacket on and fastened the belt as well. "Seriously, though, thank you. This is awesome."

"You're welcome. Now let's go stake your first vampire." Grady made to leave.

"Wait. What?"

"There was more to this routine appointment with Dacey, I'm afraid. I was hoping he'd confess a secret. He did. Unfortunately, it was the wrong one."

"You're going to make me kill Dacey?" Ethan's heart plummeted. He'd just met the guy, stared into his eyes, and now he was going to hunt him down and kill him? He'd never killed anything before. Not even a goldfish.

"Goodness no!" Grady answered. "Well...unless you want to."

"No!" Ethan scoffed.

Grady appeared far too amused by his reaction.

Grady filled him in as they left the office. "Information came my way that a vampire had turned someone. We're going on a stakeout—*love* that pun by the way—to the cemetery to see if it's true. If it is, this new creature will rise from the grave and you'll have your first lesson in vampire hunting." He grabbed a long dark-brown double-breasted trench coat of his own. Ethan wondered what items filled the lining of Grady's newest favored jacket.

"Wait. You're leaving already?" Vivian asked from the front desk. Benny glanced up from writing something in a file with a Sharpie. At least, that's what it seemed like he was doing. Ethan was fairly certain he'd just been standing there sniffing it.

"Yes, I'm afraid we must," Grady answered shortly, heading for the door.

Vivian stood and waved a stack of various-colored sticky notes at them. "But you have calls waiting to be returned! And an appointment later with Wailing Walter."

"Wailing Walter." Grady moaned. "Didn't I see him at the beginning of the week? What on earth does he want from me now? No. Never mind. I don't want to know. Tell him I'm ill. Tell them all I'm ill and I'll deal with them tomorrow."

Vivian sat down in a huff and began to call the clients to reschedule.

"Who's Wailing Walter?" Ethan asked as they left the office. The sun was going down as they got into Grady's car.

"An *asos si*." Seeing Ethan's puzzled expression, he clarified. "A banshee."

"I thought banshees were girls."

"For the most part, they're female. Rarely, you'll happen upon a male. Walter is one of the most tiresome creatures I've yet to deal with," Grady said, as they drove away. "He doesn't seem to realize his condition is meant to stand as an omen and instead utilizes it as a form of melodramatics."

"So, he's a big cry baby?"

Grady smiled. "Precisely."

"AGAIN!" GRADY INSTRUCTED.

Ethan gripped the stake tight in his right hand and stabbed forward with it. In one fluid motion, Grady grabbed his wrist and pulled his arm behind him.

"Ugh! I suck at this," Ethan lamented.

It was after dark and the two men were waiting next to a fresh grave in the cemetery. Grady was giving Ethan a crash course in grappling with a vampire.

"Have *you* ever watched any films about vampire hunting?" Grady asked.

Ethan nodded. "Yes, lots."

"That's your problem, then. You'll want to forget everything you've seen. This isn't a place for theatrics. You're thinking too much. You won't look like an action hero. It's more primal than that."

"Okay." Ethan shook it off.

"Be observant," Grady advised. "When you search in front of you, try to see everything all at once. You have to guess their move before they even make it."

Ethan frowned. "That's impossible."

Grady tapped him on the chest, indicating his heart. "Not if the only thing you hear *here* is the will to survive. Now, try again."

Ethan steadied himself.

Grady lunged at him. Instinctively, Ethan knelt down on one knee, spun the stake so the blunt end was outward facing, and slammed it firmly against Grady's chest.

Grady smiled. "Much better."

"Should we try it again?" Ethan asked, standing.

Grady sat down on a nearby bench.

"No. You should save your energy for the real thing."

Ethan joined him on the bench and tucked the stake safely into his jacket.

"You'll back me up, though, right?"

"As best I can, but I imagine I'll have my hands full with its sire."

Ethan stared toward the fresh grave, waiting anxiously for any signs of movement. He read the name on the headstone. *Jeremy Donovan.*

"You mean Dacey? He'll show up?" Ethan asked nervously.

"No, not Dacey. But whomever did sire this one will come to pluck them up when it's time."

"How do you know it wasn't Dacey? Is he that well-behaved?"

Grady chuckled. "Dacey is far from well-behaved. Surely you garnered that much from our meeting. He's predictable, and he only wants to sire one person in particular. I know it wasn't him."

"Who's the one person?"

"Me. He asks every time. It's a relentless proposal. I don't know if he honestly thinks I'll go along with it someday or if he enjoys the feeling of rejection."

"Probably both. He might think you're playing hard to get."

Grady just hummed in response.

Ethan glanced at Grady with discreet curiosity. He had already learned so much about the man, and yet, in a way, he still didn't know him at all. He wanted to know more, but was afraid to ask.

"What is it then?" Ethan finally asked after he'd worked up the courage. "Between you and Dacey? You said it's not a real relationship."

Grady fell silent.

"It's an arrangement?" Ethan suggested when it became clear Grady wasn't going to answer.

"More like an understanding," Grady said softly.

"He understands you?" His stomach was uneasy. He wasn't sure why, but the idea anyone could understand Grady made him jealous.

"As best he can, anyway. Don't get the wrong idea, Ethan. What Dacey and I share isn't something anyone should aspire to. It's heartless and it's vulgar. We're both dancing with death when we're together, and that, I suppose, is the appeal for both of us."

"Because you could kill each other at any moment just as easily." Ethan realized the horror of what Grady was confiding in him. Now he was sick to his stomach in an entirely different way.

"He could kill me, yes. And I could destroy him. Technically, he's already dead," Grady continued. "That's how we remain different. I'm human. He's not. I endure the pain he causes me as a test of prowess and stamina. But the pain I cause him...he truly *revels* in it. The monster comes out to play."

"That sounds..." Ethan started to say something, but then he became far too self-aware that he couldn't control the flushing of his cheeks again.

"Dysfunctional." Grady sighed with shame.

"I was going to say kinky, but sure, dysfunctional works too." Ethan smiled at him. He couldn't imagine the physical or emotional torture Grady must have endured in his life, and he was sure he didn't want to.

"Let's not speak of Dacey anymore tonight. I'm sure he's not spending his time thinking about us." Grady sat straight again, his attention returned to the grave and their surroundings.

"What about Marguerite? What happened there?"

"You know, you've asked an awful lot of questions about my personal life, and yet I know nothing of yours." He smiled at Ethan and raised his eyebrows.

Ethan shrugged. "I don't really have one to speak of. Sorry."

"But you have had one?" Grady prodded. "Some ex-girlfriend with a broken heart?"

Ethan smirked. "Hardly."

"No ex-girlfriend?"

"Not really into girls," Ethan admitted. "And no, no exes. No currents. No anything. I've always been just me."

"I see." Grady patted him on the knee. "Probably for the best, really. People complicate things."

"And vampires?" Ethan teased.

Grady smiled. "They're the worst complications of all."

Something stirred underground near them. Grady's attention locked on the plot and Ethan's pulse escalated. He reached inside his jacket and rested his hand on the wooden stake at the ready.

Ethan was unprepared for the quickness of it all. Within a breath, arms broke upward from the ground with unnatural ease. The dirt caved in as the head and torso of a man emerged. His eyes were a wild yellow, and when he saw them, he bared fresh fangs and hissed.

Grady was already on his feet but facing the wrong direction. Ethan froze for a moment, bewildered. What was he doing?

That was Ethan's mistake. He shouldn't have questioned it. He glanced over his shoulder to see what Grady was up to and the new vampire ran forward to attack.

The sire, a female with piercing green eyes and short strawberry hair, burst forth from the shadows. Grady was already set to face her.

Ethan was toppled over by the new vampire. He cried out in fear, unable to pull the stake from his jacket.

Grady glanced over and gave a swift kick to the vampire crouching over Ethan, sending him rolling off a few feet. The other vampire jumped on Grady with her fangs bared, trying to bite at his neck, but he caught her by the throat and struggled free.

Ethan managed to stand, pull the stake out, and hop onto the bench, hoping the slight elevation would give him some sort of advantage. He glanced to Grady as the two fought. Grady knocked her to the ground and whipped out a silver cross, pressing it into her forehead while she screamed in agony.

The new vampire instantly became protective of her and fixed his sights on Grady, rushing toward him.

Ethan took the opportunity and jumped onto the vampire. He attempted to stake him, but the vampire shook him off and the stake rolled away. With Ethan down and unarmed, the vampire smiled wickedly at his easy prey.

"Run," Grady shouted. The female vampire used the momentary distraction to force Grady off of herself.

Ethan scrambled to his feet in an effort to escape but found he'd injured his ankle when he'd landed. The pain hit him like wildfire, and he crumpled onto the ground. He was sure to die.

In a fluid motion, Grady reached into his long brown jacket and produced two khukuri knives. He quickly crossed his wrists and swiped out around the female vampire's throat. Their inwardly curved blades severed her head with ease, and her body fell limp to the ground.

The remaining vampire lunged at Ethan with his fangs out, ready to rip through his neck.

"No!" Grady shouted.

Ethan reached out his right palm toward the vampire, as if it could shield him, and closed his eyes. Then something strange happened. Nothing.

Curious, Ethan opened his eyes, wondering why he wasn't dead yet. The air around him had become visible in a manner that simulated water or a translucent gelatinous matter. The vampire had hit this magical barrier and was unable to reach him. In a swift motion, he was decapitated. His body fell limply to the earth while his head rolled toward him until it hit the barrier and stopped still, staring at Ethan eerily. Grady was the only one left standing. He calmly wiped the blades of his knife off with his handkerchief and replaced them in his jacket.

"H-how...how did I do that?" Ethan stuttered, shaking with fear and confusion on the cold dirt.

"*I* did that," Grady stated evenly.

"No. The other thing," Ethan said, holding out his palms as if they had somehow betrayed him.

Grady's face was now lined with concern and something else Ethan hadn't seen before. He could swear it was awe.

Grady took Ethan's hand and pulled him to his feet.

"There *may* have been a specific reason Arthur sent you to me," Grady finally confessed.

Twelve: Bring Me a Dream

"I THOUGHT YOU said you wouldn't look like an action hero," Ethan said as he reclined on a hunter-green antique lounge couch in Grady's study.

Vivian was attending to his injured ankle. It was slightly fractured so Grady had called her over to attempt a healing spell. Her boyfriend, Thomas, who was hovering over them to watch, had accompanied her, much to Grady's chagrin.

"I said *you* wouldn't look like an action hero," Grady said. He had taken to pacing around the area in contemplation while Vivian worked. Benny, now in the form of the little brown Chihuahua, followed in his steps.

She ran her hands repeatedly over Ethan's ankle with her eyes closed while she murmured an incantation that sounded like gibberish to Ethan.

"I don't see why he was even there to begin with," Thomas huffed. "The poor kid could've been killed."

"But he wasn't," Grady retorted. His flippant answer sparked outrage in Thomas, and he moved around the sofa to confront him.

Ethan spoke up. "I'm okay. Really!"

Thomas ignored him and planted himself directly in front of Grady, blocking the imaginary path Grady had been forging for the past several minutes.

"You're completely reckless. What were you thinking?" Thomas demanded.

Benny barked protectively.

"I'm entirely sure none of this is your business," Grady said, straightening and standing his ground.

"You make it my business when you bring my girlfriend into it." Thomas crossed his arms and stared Grady square in the eyes.

"She was my friend before she was your girlfriend."

Thomas let out a sarcastic laugh. "Your friend. Is that right? Doctor Grady Hunter doesn't have friends. He has pawns and enemies. Tell me, which category does Ethan fit in to? Or have you not decided yet?"

Grady crossed his arms. "I think you should leave."

"And if I don't? Then what? What will you do?" Thomas countered.

Grady didn't respond but instead seemed to watch Thomas calculatingly.

Thomas sneered. "Will you hit me? Will you stab me? Will you try to kill me? I'm not one of your little monsters. You have no dominion over me. And for that matter, you have none over any of them either, as much as you love to think that you do."

Vivian opened her eyes as she completed her work. She pushed away the strands of her black bobbed hair, which had fallen into her face, and peered over to the two men as if she'd only just noticed what was going on. Ethan was watching them with great interest as well.

She picked up a cup of tea the ghostly Agatha had brought in earlier and pulled a small package of some indistinct herb out of her purse and gently poured it into the cup. She stirred it with a spoon from the tea tray and handed it to Ethan.

"He'll be fine," she announced loudly as a way to inadvertently break up the argument. "It won't be completely healed for a few days, but it'll be a much faster process than with traditional medicine."

She smiled kindly at him. "The tea will help, so drink it up. And while you should be able to move around, I don't think it would be wise to go chasing any vampires again soon. You'll probably want to avoid dancing at the Halloween party too."

"No dancing? I'm bereft." Ethan feigned sorrow and then smiled at her as he took a sip of the tea.

Vivian made her way over to Grady and Thomas.

Grady nodded to her with appreciation.

"Thank you, Viv."

"Of course. Make sure he drinks all of the tea. It'll help ease the pain."

Grady glanced to Ethan who was guzzling the tea down fine.

"You drugged him?" he asked with suspicion.

She smiled coyly. "Nothing I haven't given you before."

"That's what I'm afraid of." He seemed amused.

"You keep that kid out of danger from now on," Thomas said, sticking a warning finger into Grady's chest. "Or you'll have me to answer to."

Grady glared contemptuously at him. "I answer to no one." Grady glared contemptuously at him.

"That's the problem."

Grady swallowed his pride and didn't respond further.

"Let's go," Thomas said to Vivian as he glowered at Grady.

"I hope your ankle heals soon," he said kindly to Ethan.

Ethan smiled blissfully. The tea had obviously kicked in.

"See you tomorrow," Vivian whispered sweetly to Grady before she and Thomas made their exit.

"Goodnight," Grady said simply. He waited until the front door to the house shut before he turned to Ethan.

Benny curled by the fireplace now they had the house to themselves.

"I don't know what she sees in him." Grady repeated his sentiment from earlier in the evening as he took a seat on the sofa next to Ethan.

"He has big muscles. I think she likes that," Ethan mused.

"They're not that big," Grady grumbled.

Ethan grinned dreamily. "Yeah they are. He looks like Superman."

Grady glanced at him reproachfully and then laughed.

"He does kind of have a Clark Kent thing going on, I suppose," he admitted.

"And really big muscles." Ethan sighed, resting back onto the couch.

The corners of Grady's lips twitched. "Yes, I think you covered that already." But his amusement quickly faded as the gravity of the situation returned to him.

"I wanted to talk to you about what happened earlier."

"You mean my magic shield? That *was* pretty cool." Ethan giggled.

Grady gave him an appraising look. "Perhaps we should wait to discuss it tomorrow when you've sobered up."

"Will it be easier for me to accept then?"

"Probably not, but at least I know you'll remember what I've said." Grady turned in his seat to face Ethan, resting his elbow on the back of the lounge sofa.

"It's okay. Give it to me straight, Doc," Ethan joked. "What am I? A witch? A superhero?"

It took Grady a moment to decide how to answer. "Have you ever heard of the Sandman?"

"*Bring me a dream,*" Ethan sang whimsically.

Grady smiled sweetly at him. "Yes."

"You mean the guy who puts sand in people's eyes?"

"Folklore and pop culture have a way of exaggerating things." He took a deep breath before continuing.

"The Sandman, or *Ole Lukøje* as Hans Christian Andersen once deemed him, was a creature of the dream world. It is a separate reality from our own, which can be accessed when we sleep. For most, it's nothing more than their individual imaginations allow. For the supernatural set, it's an actual place where real events transpire. However, the only way you could gain passage to this wondrous reality was to either be born there or led there by a *Somnium Viator*."

"Insomnia gator?"

"*Somnium Viator*, Dream Traveler. It's what I believe you may be," Grady confessed. "Arthur suspected it also, which is why he sent you to me. He wants me to protect you."

"Protect me from what?" Ethan sat a little straighter, concern lining his face.

"Everything. As legend tells, the Sandman came to our world and took the form of a human. He could manipulate the dreams of men; he could even take them into the dream world with him if he chose to. He was one of a kind. A true legendary creature. A deity, if you like to believe in such a way."

Ethan frowned. "Was?"

"Legend has it he produced a half-human lineage. These children were the Dream Travelers," Grady continued. "But you know humans. They hate what they don't understand, and if they *do* understand it, they seek to profit from it. Imagine what you could do if you controlled someone who could access the dream world at will. Someone who can alter reality for those around them."

Ethan pulled his knees against his chest. He suddenly looked very vulnerable to Grady.

Grady took a deep breath and pressed on. "The Sandman was eventually destroyed, believed by mankind to be a demon. His lineage was mostly wiped from existence. I hate to say it, but even that dream catcher I offered you, the one you find comfort in, was a weapon against your kind. It was created to bind you, which is why you won't dream when you have it. For now, I thought it wise to use as a tool to help you, at least until you can learn to control your transitions yourself."

"So...there are others? Like me?" Ethan asked hopefully.

"No," he answered. "No. I'm afraid, if our research is correct, you are the last. It's why your father asked Arthur to make sure you stayed protected."

"It was my father," Ethan said slowly as he worked it out.

"As far as Arthur has told me, your mother never even knew. She's not aware of the supernatural world at all. Your father thought it best she not know the truth," Grady said softly, resting his hand on Ethan's shoulder to comfort him.

Ethan grew quiet and stared at the floor. Grady remained supportive and let him take all the time he needed.

"I can't believe Arthur never told me," Ethan said after several minutes had passed.

"He was doing what he felt was best. He had promised your father."

"So he sends me off to a complete stranger to do the dirty work," Ethan spat, but his anger was short-lived. "Sorry, you're not a stranger now. I mean, it seems cowardly of him."

Grady nodded his concurrence.

"I'm sure he viewed me as more able to have this conversation. He would have been too emotional."

"You know, growing up, everyone always had such nice things to say about my dad. I guess that's what you do for a kid whose dad died before he even got a chance to know him. You tell them they were the greatest guy ever," Ethan said. "But keeping a secret like that from my mom... How could he do that? It's like...damning someone you love. She didn't even have the opportunity to choose if she wanted a freak for a son!"

"You're not a freak, Ethan."

"A monster then! A demon. Whatever people want to label it," Ethan said angrily. "I'm not human. Not fully. And if she didn't know, how could she have been properly equipped to protect me?"

"Honestly, I agree with you, but I'm sure your father thought he'd be the one to bear that burden. And if not him, then he trusted Arthur. Arthur knew the truth about him all along."

"It's so messed up they didn't tell her." He took a moment to groggily process it all. "What's done is done. I survived. I'm an adult now. My problems are my own. Not hers or Arthur's."

Grady gave him an approving nod. "That's very wise."

Ethan sighed. "This is terrible."

Grady cocked his head. "Why do you say that?"

"It's a curse."

"No, a curse is what Benny deals with. This is who you are."

"Even worse. It means there's no escaping it." Ethan slumped into the couch again.

"Hell of a responsibility too," he added. "The only one left in existence? That means if I die before I have kids, I've failed my entire species. Oh, but here's the kicker, *I have to have kids*! Which in my case means I have to do things out of an obligation to my race, not because it has anything to do with who I am or what I want in life."

"You don't owe anything to anyone." Grady squeezed his shoulder. "The choice is yours alone and you have no one to answer to for it. If you are to be the last of your kind, that is for you alone to decide, and if you *do* choose that, it was meant to be as such."

Ethan's eyes swelled with tears now, and he stared at Grady pleadingly. "Tell me I'm hallucinating from Vivian's pain medication! Tell me this is all a bad dream."

"I'm sorry, Ethan," was all Grady could offer.

Ethan went limp with defeat and leaned into Grady, who embraced him and let him rest there as he wept.

Once the tears stopped, Ethan's voice was hollow as he laid his head against Grady's chest.

"Of course. It only makes sense my life would be a series of bad dreams." Ethan said dully, almost more to himself than to Grady.

"Life in its essence is tragic," Grady said softly.

The two sat on the lounge chair together, staring in contemplation at the flames that flickered in the fireplace. It was well after midnight, and Benny had already fallen asleep on the rug before them. His nose twitched from time to time as he dreamed.

"We're born oblivious to the circumstances we'll face. In that way, everything has the potential to mar us," he continued, "but...there are those times life isn't so tragic. It can be a comedy, a romance, or an adventure. We don't get to choose the mediums we compose our life with, but we can choose to paint it in whatever way we like. We make our own destiny with whatever tools we have on hand. For all the horrors of life, there are also the times we can treasure. That's one thing you can take Dacey's word for. You should enjoy the good things in life while they're around so that you have something to hold onto during the hard times."

"Do you take your own advice?" Ethan wondered.

Grady took a moment to respond.

"I suppose I wouldn't know," he finally answered. "I haven't known anything good for a very long time."

Ethan sat up to consider him.

"How do you do it then? How do you keep going when you see nothing but pain ahead of you?"

"I suppose the virtuous answer is hope. At least, I would wish that were the motivation. The idea I'm working toward something better for the world and for myself. In reality, I think it's distraction. I've created enough *missions* and surrounded myself with enough people to watch out for, that I don't really have time to think of myself anymore."

Ethan bit his lip. "Am I just another distraction?"

"No," Grady answered. "You're not a distraction. You're my priority."

"But for the same reason? Someone to protect."

Grady shook his head. "I thought that at first. But now it's something more."

Ethan wiped the last tears from his eyes and smiled.

"If everything you told me is true, which I have no reason to believe it isn't...then it looks like I'm here for the long haul."

Grady returned his smile. "Yes, it does appear that way. I hope the house is to your liking."

"It is," Ethan said. "But I wasn't talking about the house. I was talking about us. This. Our unique friendship. You seem pretty honor bound to protect me, and in truth, I owe you for saving my life. Whatever happens from here on out, we're in it together. Neither one of us ever has to feel alone."

Grady felt something warm in his chest—it almost felt like happiness.

"We make our own destiny, right?" Ethan continued, clearly warming up to the idea. "Like you said. We'll do it together, and we'll find a way to make our lives happy no matter how much bad shit gets thrown at us."

"And when that doesn't work anymore? When one of us dies? What then?"

Ethan took him by the hand and squeezed it tight. "We don't let that happen."

Ethan leaned forward in an attempt to kiss him.

Grady pressed his hand firmly on Ethan's chest, blocking any advance. Ethan pulled back, blinking in bewilderment.

"I can't," Grady said gently. "You've had a rough night."

Ethan wrapped his arms around himself, the hurt radiating from him. Grady cursed inwardly—as if the poor boy hadn't been through enough.

Grady took his hand. "I will promise you something, though, Ethan. I won't see Dacey anymore. Not about anything other than business, anyway."

"It doesn't matter," Ethan said. "Do whatever you want."

"That is what I want," Grady insisted. "You inspire me to be better. No matter what this becomes between you and me. If it remains friendship or if it evolves into something else entirely... Dacey is a sickness to me and this is my opportunity to rid myself of it. You're my witness. You'll help keep me strong?"

"Of course," Ethan swore. Grady knew the scales were never tipped in Ethan's favor and the weight of his own advantage suddenly felt crushing. "I know your secrets, Ethan. I knew them before you did. That's very unfair. I want to share my secret with you. No one else knows, and telling you is the first action in my resolve to stop this madness of mine."

Ethan peered at him, "What are you talking about?"

Grady unbuttoned his shirt and threw it to the floor, revealing the scars on his torso. They told of old instances of torture, and some were fresh cuts still healing. They lined his chest, his abdomen, and his sides. One thing, though, stood out amongst all of them. Fresh bite marks. They were right above his beltline, near his left hip. Fangs.

"That was Dacey?" Ethan gaped with horror. "All of it?"

"I told you. It's a sickness," Grady confirmed. "I've had no one else in a very long time. Least of all anyone who actually cared for me. That's not an excuse, but it's what led me to him. For the past year, I've been living in complete recklessness when it comes to myself. I suppose part of me hoped Dacey would end it all. Of course, he loves playing with me. I'm nothing but another trivial amusement to him. One he can tinker with on a whim. But not anymore."

He took Ethan's hand again. "I have you now. We're in this together for as long as it lasts, just like you said. I'll take my own advice and know to enjoy something good when I have it."

Ethan flushed a little, and a smile danced upon his lips. Grady couldn't help but smile back. This moment of connection was worth so much more than a sloppy, drunken kiss.

"I don't know about you, but I'm not sleepy in the least," Grady said, bringing the tone of the conversation to a casual place.

"Any suggestions on how to pass the time?" Ethan's meaning was transparent.

Grady laughed.

"I was thinking of painting tonight. It helps me center myself. You could keep me company if you like."

"You could paint me!" Ethan stood and threw his arms out in a silly pose. Ethan whipped around and peered at the piano. He hobbled over to it and sat down.

"Yes! Paint me playing a song." Ethan tickled a few of the keys.

Grady laughed and stood to gather his supplies. "All right. You've got it."

It was with a carefree bliss, despite the impending terrors life could quickly provide them, that Ethan played Bach, and Chopin, and Brahms into the late hours of the night and early morning. Grady painted Ethan as the new muse who had been thrust into his life in that unexpected way that affects things that have a taste of destiny to them. The horrors the morning daylight and a lifetime ahead of them might bring could wait. Tonight, they had their artistry, their passion, and, above all, their friendship.

Thirteen: Costumes & Alibis

IT WASN'T UNTIL afternoon that Ethan finally awoke and came down from his room. He found both Grady and Benny in the study. Grady was at his desk, staring at his laptop and absentmindedly rubbing his right temple as he immersed himself in reading, while Benny sat on the lounge sofa, where serious discussions had occurred the night before, sewing some fashion of tiny fabric pieces.

"What are you up to?" Ethan wondered, joining Benny on the couch. Benny held his project with self-satisfaction. It was a tiny green costume that would only be big enough to fit a small dog.

"It's for the Halloween party!" Benny grinned. "I'm going as the Incredible Hulk. I figure I have a few things in common with him."

"Oh yeah," Ethan said, realizing a couple of things at once. "You'll be a Chihuahua at the party. Well, I think the Hulk is a great choice. Nice handiwork. I guess I need to throw something together. I hadn't even thought about a costume yet. I've had too much going on."

"Well, we're closed since it's Devil's Night. You could run to a Halloween store and grab something," Benny suggested. "I like making my own. There's not many human things I'm good at, but crafts seem to be one of them."

Ethan frowned at Grady. "We're closed tonight? But isn't Devil's Night supposed to be a night of mischief? Wouldn't things be super busy?"

Grady casually glanced up from his computer. "That's a misnomer. Devil's Night has nothing to do with monsters. It's a night generally for human mischief, so if there are any problems, that's for the police to contend with. It came into existence in the 1930s precisely because of the actions of human youth during that time. For the supernatural, it's a dead night. Pun entirely intended."

"We're all too busy planning for the real night," Benny interjected. "All Hallows Eve! Samhain!"

"Costume parties." Ethan smiled.

"Costume parties," Benny cheered.

"What does a ghost wear to a costume party?" Ethan wondered aloud. "Do monsters get offended if you dress up as them?"

"Do monsters get offended?" Grady snorted. "Listen to yourself. What a silly sentiment. No, I should guess monsters don't take offense to much."

"All right then," Ethan said, coming to a decision. "I'll try to go find something to wear later. Which I will segue into another question. When do we get paid? Or do we get paid?"

Grady frowned at Benny. "You didn't give it to him?"

"Oops!" Benny blushed, quickly reached into his back pocket, and pulled out his wallet. He took out a credit card and handed it over to Ethan.

"I was supposed to give this to you when I trained you your first day," Benny said. "Totally slipped my mind what with all the getting to know you and cleaning the graveyard dirt and stuff."

Grady elevated an eyebrow. "Graveyard dirt?"

Benny's eyes grew wide as he realized he'd told on himself. He started laughing nervously. "Graveyard dirt? What are you talking about? No one said anything about any graveyard dirt, you silly moose."

"Goose," Ethan corrected.

"No one said anything about a graveyard goose either," Benny added. "Anyway, this is yours and the only rule Grady has is not to spend over five thousand dollars a month. Unless you absolutely need to for some reason. In which case, run it by him first."

Ethan turned to Grady with shock. "Is he for real?"

"I've learned it's easier for me to keep my employees happy and compliant if they feel they have the ability to get whatever they could want or need. Generally, no one ever spends anywhere near that much and it saves me from dealing with the tedious mundane task of a payroll," Grady answered as a matter of fact.

"What about taxes?"

"For all intents and purposes, and to anyone non-supernatural who asks, you are unemployed. You let me worry about my side of things."

Ethan shrugged and slipped the card into his pocket at the same moment his phone started ringing. He pulled it out and stared at the screen.

"Ugh, it's my mom." He rose. "Excuse me. I'm going to take this out in the hall."

"Wait!" Grady said, startled. "You can't answer that!"

"Why not? I haven't been answering her calls or texts for days. I can't avoid her forever," Ethan replied, stopping in his tracks.

"What are you going to say?" Grady was looking at him with unusual intensity.

"I don't know." Ethan shrugged. "I need to let her know I'm fine. I'm sure she's been freaking out."

"She'll start asking questions," Grady countered. "Where have you been? What have you been up to? Do you have any solid answers for those questions? Because you can't tell her the truth, and if it remotely sounds like you're making anything up, she'll know it."

The phone stopped ringing and went to voice mail.

"I have to talk to her at some point," Ethan argued. "I can't keep ignoring her."

"Can't you?" Grady asked hopefully.

Ethan frowned at him, unamused.

"I'll tell her I moved in with a friend and I've been busy. That's all."

"Oh, yes, because mothers are so keen on vague explanations. I'm sure she'll fully accept that and never ask you about it again." Grady rolled his eyes. "The situation as it stands, ignoring the paranormal aspect, is that you've moved into a large house with a seemingly wealthy man twenty years your elder, who also happens to be boarding another young man. You've stopped attending classes and are avoiding your family and friends. If she's privy to any one of those details, she will invariably *freak out*, as you call it. Besides, now that I've said it, it makes me sound like a lecherous manipulative cad. No, you can't tell her anything."

"So? You're not my sugar daddy?" Ethan teased, holding the credit card with a mischievous smirk.

This time it was Grady's turn to frown in annoyance.

Ethan gave in. "Fine. I'll wait until I have a good alibi put together before I talk to her."

"Thank you. I'll play along with whatever you decide," Grady said, clearly satisfied he'd gotten his way. He returned his attention to the screen before him.

Ethan walked to the desk and leaned over Grady's shoulder to see what he'd been so immersed in. Grady had several windows open and was clicking back and forth between them. One was obviously his email, but the rest, Ethan couldn't identify. A few of the screens were documents, some had black-and-white ink illustrations of people, one window had a timeline that consisted of names and dates, and another window had a map with various colored pinpoints labeling it.

"Doing some research?" Ethan guessed.

"In a sense. More like detective work. That vampire we fought last night, the female, wasn't one of ours. Not a Shady Pines native, so to speak. I've never seen her before, and Dacey insists he has no idea who she was either, which is troubling because he always knows everyone worth knowing…and if she was here siring new vampires, then she was definitely worth knowing. I'm trying to see if I can trace where she came from, who she was, and most importantly, why she was here."

Ethan's jaw clenched slightly at the mention of the vampire's name. "You talked to Dacey today?"

Grady must have sensed his jealous tone and answered simply. "Through a text, and I kept it on topic."

Embarrassed for even asking, especially since Benny was eying them far too intently, Ethan cleared his throat and moved on.

"What are those?" He pointed to the window with the pinpoints.

"Locations of supernatural entities in our area and surrounding cities. Color coded by species." As he hovered the cursor over different points, a small description box came up, giving the name, species, and physical address associated with each creature.

"That's handy."

"Indeed. It's something I've been developing and has proved extremely useful thus far."

"Is there anything I can help with?"

"No, I'm afraid for now the trail might be lost. I have a few other contacts I can inquire on the subject, but I don't need any help with that. You should go out. Enjoy the daylight for once. It's not healthy to only live at night."

"I do think I need some fresh air...and that costume. Benny, you want to come along?"

Benny jumped at the chance to get out of the house.

"Of course! I actually have some great costume ideas for you!"

"I'm sure you do." Ethan smiled as they headed out.

Benny hesitated at the door for a moment. "Grady, will you be here later? Or are you still going to Dacey's?"

Ethan glanced at Grady, curious to find out his response.

Grady smiled politely at them. "I'll be here."

"Yes! I hate when you go over there. That guy gets my hackles up," Benny responded with relief. "You always come back out of sorts."

"Don't worry, Benny. That won't be a problem any longer," Grady assured him.

They waved their goodbyes, but Grady was already immersed in his research.

The Mechanics of Sleep Travel

Excerpts from The Mechanics of Sleep Travel *by Dr. Arthur Ellis*

VII. As the subject's corporal form remains tethered to its world of origin, the spirit can project temporarily into other realms but must be recalled to its source. The subject should create a verbal or auditory anchor in their point of origin to consciously guide themselves back at will.

VIII. The astral form can take shape as a mirrored image of itself elsewhere and experience all senses completely. It can interact and be interacted with. All instances of experience that occur remotely concurrently occur with the original body—including death.

IX. The "Dream World" is essentially the first stop on an expressway to every world in every dimension that the traveler seeks admittance to. The more experienced a traveler becomes, the more easily they can access the portals to their desired destinations.

*X. Subjects may guide other entities across realms and even return with them to their point of origin if the guest is in physical contact when the subject recalls themselves or chooses to travel.***

***The implications of bringing foreign entities to new realms is an affront to the natural order of the multiverse. Due to past occurrences, it has been declared an act of ultimate moral corruption and multiversally banned. This act is extremely dangerous, and the author advises that it should never be practically applied.*

Fourteen: Devil's Night

IT WAS AFTER dark when Ethan and Benny finally made it home. They had spent the day doing exactly what Grady had prescribed, enjoying the sunlight. Ethan had taken Benny around to some of his favorite parts of town—ones Benny had never had a chance to visit before. They walked around the Japanese Botanical Garden and they visited the fine art museum, which Ethan quickly learned wasn't the best idea with Benny's hyperactive personality. They had chicken fajitas at Ethan's favorite restaurant, Rodrigo's, and of course, they found the perfect costume for Ethan at one of the local Halloween stores.

It was good to do something normal for a change, Ethan had thought. He was refreshed and Benny was having so much fun they lost track of the time and barely made it on the road home before Benny transformed. Ethan vowed he'd never intentionally witness it again and definitely not while he was trying to drive. There were certain horrors to the process Ethan wouldn't mind washing away with a strong drink and he wasn't even the drinking type.

As they ascended the stairs to their respective rooms, Ethan's hands full with their purchases from the day, Grady peeked out of his own room to greet them.

"I didn't expect you'd stay out that late." He didn't seem upset, however, but rather distracted.

"Just lost track of time," Ethan said, and Benny barked in confirmation before scampering off to his own room.

"No worries. Put your things away and then come here. I've got something to show you," Grady said happily and then disappeared into his room, leaving the door open.

Ethan's curiosity was piqued, so he quickly threw his bags onto his bed and ventured to see what the other man was up to.

Grady's room was twice the size of Ethan's, though decorated the same as the rest of the house. Crimson silk curtains were pulled back to reveal there was also a set of french doors, which were currently open and letting a breeze waft in. They led to a balcony facing the rear of the house. This is where Ethan found Grady, leaning against the aged white-stone balustrade, staring down at the dahlia garden below.

Before Ethan could even ask what Grady wanted to show him, the faint sound of music came from nearby. It was emanating from the lower level of the house. A window must have been open somewhere, and Ethan's educated ears picked up Mendelssohn was playing, bringing a pleased curve to his lips.

"Do you see it?" Grady asked in a low whisper as if he were afraid someone might hear them.

At first, Ethan thought he meant the beauty of the garden, but then he spotted them. Ethan joined Grady in leaning forward on the banister to watch the haunting sight closely. It was absolutely beautiful.

The ghosts of Agatha and John were waltzing in the far end of the garden, hovering above the mauve dahlias, with the nearly full moon adding an eerie but gorgeous lighting to the scene. Ethan fell speechless to the spectacle.

"They're absolutely stunning," Ethan finally managed to whisper.

"Aren't they?" Grady grinned. "I wish they would dance every night. It's a peaceful thing to witness. It always brings me a sense of hope...but maybe that's because I'm hopeless."

Ethan smirked. "A hopeless romantic, maybe." Ethan smirked.

Grady sighed. "I actually wish that were true, but I meant it as I said it." Grady sighed.

"You're way too hard on yourself," Ethan said. "But you're right about them. It does give you hope. There's proof right before us that even after the looming threat of death has passed, our spirits can still find something worth rejoicing in."

Grady gave a soft laugh. "Don't go waxing poetic on me, Ethan. I may never recover." Grady gave a soft laugh.

Ethan beamed and stole a glance at him. With the moonlight gracing his face, Ethan thought Grady was easily reminiscent of a Renaissance sculpture. It was as if Michelangelo had created the statue of David someplace out of time and Grady was his muse. Shadows danced in all the right angles upon his face. Ethan grasped the railing tighter as if he could anchor his thoughts from carrying him into the clouds.

"I wonder what makes some stay and others go," Ethan mused, returning his attention to the spirits in an effort to maintain a level head. "Why don't we all stay as ghosts?"

"Everyone wonders that, and I suppose no one will ever know. It's an enigma that has always fascinated me. When I lost Ava..."

Grady took a deep breath and paused for a moment before he continued. "They say a soul sticks around because of unfinished business or a violent death that shocks them. I don't believe that. Ava had both of those reasons to stay, but she didn't. Believe me, I searched for her spirit. I engaged in many séances and rituals, hoping to find her. Traveled the world in an effort to reach her. I never received any answer. It angered me for a very long time, the idea she *chose* to leave me behind. That's completely selfish, I know. Don't worry. I crossed that bridge a long time ago and made peace with it. I'm happy she crossed over. The hope I have now is she's somewhere better instead of stuck here in this godforsaken place with the rest of our lot."

"My guess is our experiences with death are as unique to us as our experiences with life."

"That's probably the best theory I've heard so far," Grady agreed.

"You think she's in Heaven?" Ethan asked gently.

"I don't pretend to know where they go. I hope it's better than where they've been." Grady stared at the moon as if it might confirm this.

"You don't believe in God?" Ethan wondered.

"I have no use for religion."

Ethan smirked with mild disbelief. "Really? You believe in everything else but not that?"

"I believe in the things I've seen. I believe in my own realm of experience," Grady said. "I've never seen anything that made me think a god exists. Honestly, the closest thing I've ever seen to proof of such a construct, of God, is you. You're something greater than us all and not entirely of this world."

He locked on to Ethan's gaze and studied the surprise that washed over him. Ethan silently thanked the shadows of the night for hiding his blush this time.

"Now *that's* poetic. And, I'm afraid, entirely unearned on my part." Ethan shifted his weight onto his left foot in a way that brought their bodies closer together.

"Really?" Grady grinned. "How many people do you know who can freely travel the stream of the universal subconscious?"

"Yeah, well, not so freely it turns out." Ethan shrugged. "I have no control over it."

"I think I can help you with that," Grady said, moving away from the railing. "Besides hunting down dead-end leads on vampires, I've also been doing some research on your situation. I'd like to try an experiment if you'd be open to it."

"Does it involve any more bodily harm? Because my ankle is finally healing and I don't think that Thomas guy would be too happy if I break anything else," Ethan teased.

"Thomas is never happy with anything that involves me. You watch, Vivian will bring him to the party tomorrow and he'll spend the entire time murdering me with his eyes," Grady said in a half-joking manner.

"As long as he's not murdering you with his hands, then you shouldn't be too worried about him," Ethan said as they headed into the house.

"I don't worry about him. He means well. He just needs to mean well about someone else is all." Grady breathed the sigh of a lost cause and then his phone rang.

"Speak of the devil," he said with surprise, holding the screen to Ethan. It was Vivian calling.

"And on Devil's Night too," Ethan added. "Must be extra foreboding."

Grady laughed and answered the phone. "What is it, love?"

"Good! I was hoping you'd answer." Vivian's voice came across loudly enough Ethan could hear. "It's Marguerite. I think she's been casting conjuring spells. I don't have any proof, but I read it in the cards."

"Your tarot readings haven't led us astray before," Grady said, his mood turning dark. "What could she be up to?"

"Who knows? But it's Marguerite, so it can't be anything good. I'm going to go by there and see if I can get her to talk to me."

"Are you sure that's wise?" Grady asked. "I could go."

"No," Vivian said quickly. "You already went once and she didn't exactly open her diary to you. She and I were best friends until...you know. I think maybe I can get through to her. I just wanted to let you know."

"All right, then," Grady said. "Let me know if you find out anything."

"I will. See you tomorrow," she said and hung up.

Ethan had sat on the edge of Grady's four-poster bed. He stared with apprehension at the concern on Grady's face.

"Everything all right?"

"I hope so," Grady said. "We'll find out soon enough, I suppose."

"So what's this experiment, Doc?"

"Have you ever been hypnotized before?" Grady asked as he grabbed a wooden chair from his desk in the corner and slid it next to the bed, then took a seat. Ethan frowned at his choice of position. He'd been hoping to coax Grady in a different direction. Directly beside him to be precise. He leaned back on his elbows and studied Grady for the hundredth time. What would it take to get him to crack?

"No," Ethan said. "That doesn't really work, does it?"

"There's an entire profession based upon it."

Ethan frowned at him pointedly. "You don't need credibility to have a profession. There are literally hundreds of professions created with insubstantial basis and questionable ethics."

Grady smirked. "I'm rubbing off on you."

"I could think of worse things…" Ethan grinned, biting his lower lip and raising his brows. He was being flirtatious, but Grady seemed unfazed.

"Which is precisely why I want to try hypnotizing you," Grady continued ardently. "You won't always have a dream catcher with you when you sleep. That would be rather impractical. I was thinking we could try to plant an anchor in your mind. Something you could use to draw yourself back whenever you wished."

"That sounds handy," Ethan agreed, completely unfocused. He had other things on his mind at the moment, and surprisingly, Grady's attempts at serious solutions to his dilemma were boring him.

Grady placed a comforting hand on Ethan's knee. This gentle action sent a jolt of nervous elation bursting into Ethan's heart, and he immediately tensed up.

"Are you all right? You seem like something is bothering you."

"I'm fine," Ethan assured him. His entire face flushed, and Grady moved to sit next to him on the bed and touched his face as if he suspected fever.

"Really, I'm fine!" Ethan insisted, completely flustered, pushing his hand away. "Stop touching me. I mean, don't stop touching me. I mean…I don't know what I mean."

Grady apparently realized what was happening and the concern faded away. He relaxed, but there was something in his eyes that embarrassed Ethan. It was pity.

"I think I know what you're going through." Grady sighed. He was obviously trying to be sympathetic, but it seemed like he was being condescending.

"You have *no* idea what I'm going through," Ethan said, falling back on the bed as he tried to avoid direct eye contact with Grady. It didn't seem to be working so he grabbed a nearby pillow and covered his face.

"No, I do," Grady insisted. "I was like you once. Young and—"

"*Don't* say naive. Say anything but naïve," Ethan muttered from under the pillow.

"Inexperienced," Grady finished.

"Seriously? You pick the one word that's worse?" Ethan huffed with disbelief and tossed the pillow aside. It wasn't helping anyway. It was a fluffy rectangle of betrayal.

"It's not a bad thing. Think of it like this. There's a plate with an eclair on it, and one person has already had plenty of sweets but the other has never tried any in their life—" Grady began awkwardly.

"Now you're saying pastries. Please, stop talking. This whole conversation is getting progressively worse."

"If it makes you feel any better, I would be lying if I said I hadn't toyed with the idea," Grady admitted. "It simply isn't appropriate."

Ethan sat up and gazed at Grady pleadingly. "*Toyed*? That's it? I've *obsessed* over it! You have no idea how I feel! And who cares about what's appropriate? There's no one here but us!"

"Ethan, calm down, you're being ridiculous."

"Don't talk down to me! Don't talk to me like we're not equals. What happened to the whole *we're in this together* thing?"

"We are, Ethan!" Grady clenched his fists. "I'm attempting to do the one thing someone who cares about you *should* be doing. I'm helping you!"

"I don't even care about that right now! What do I have to do to get you to think of me as more than just a mission?"

"Oh, goddammit, Ethan!" Grady grabbed Ethan by his cheeks and planted a firm kiss on him. Ethan was taken aback with such surprise that when Grady's warm lips parted from his, he almost thought he'd imagined the whole thing.

"Are you happy now?" Grady asked with exasperation. "Have I satisfied whatever curiosity is keeping you from maintaining your composure?"

Ethan gulped down his shock and nodded in awkward silence.

"I mean, really! You act like you've never been kissed before."

"I...I told you. I've never had anyone before," Ethan stammered, his heart still pounding so loud he could hear it. He wondered if Grady could too.

"Not even a *kiss*?"

Ethan shook his head. "That...was my first."

Grady threw his hands up in the air.

"Great! So, I've ruined *that* for you now." Grady leaned his elbows forward on his knees and rested his head in his palms in defeat.

"I wouldn't say you ruined it," Ethan said, his head still whirring. "It was actually kind of nice."

Grady considered him with pitiful eyes again. "I'm not good enough for you, Ethan. Don't you recognize that? You deserve so much better than a terrible bitter man."

Ethan moved closer to him. "Stop saying horrible things about yourself. Please. For me."

Grady let out an emotional chuckle. "*Why* do you make things so difficult?"

"Because I'm an asshole?" Ethan smiled in an attempt to recover the moment. "I'm sorry. I shouldn't have pushed you. These feelings were driving me crazy."

"Stop." Grady shook his head. "Stop apologizing, Ethan. Never apologize. You are entirely perfect. I should be the one apologizing to you. I'm sorry for being your first kiss. I know that was horrible."

"No, it wasn't." Ethan tried to assure him, but there was a hint of indecision in his response.

"Wait. Did you hesitate?"

"Well..." Ethan crinkled his nose. "It wasn't exactly what I'd expected. I mean, I always thought there would be sparks or something. Not like literal ones but like a magical feeling, you know? I thought it would be more passionate or something?"

Grady pouted as if wounded.

Ethan backtracked. "I mean, I've only had my imagination to work off of. It's not like I have any real frame of reference. For all I know, it was the best kiss ever."

Grady gave an amused snort. "No. It was terrible. I sincerely apologize."

Ethan elbowed Grady in the side. "Wow! Who knew you could be so awkward? Maybe I'm the one rubbing off on you."

"I should be so lucky." Grady grinned. His eyes had crow's feet when he smiled, which only made Ethan fall in love with him harder and faster than before.

"All right, you cheeky little thing. Now we've got *that* out of the way are you ready to do this?"

Ethan's heart flipped again. "Do what?"

"The hypnosis experiment," Grady answered as if it were obvious.

Ethan grinned. "Oh, *that*. Yes."

"Good." Grady rolled his shoulders a couple of times in an effort to regain his focus on the task he'd meant to attempt from the start. "Now, lie down and relax."

"I thought you'd never ask," Ethan teased, doing as instructed.

Grady rolled his eyes. "You'll be the undoing of me, Ethan Roam. I'm absolutely sure of it."

"I'll try, anyway," Ethan promised.

"Close your eyes, take a deep breath, and concentrate on my voice," Grady said in a calm and even tone.

Ethan shut his eyes and did as he was told. After a few moments, he became aware he'd wandered outside of himself and into a different place entirely.

IT HAPPENED MORE quickly than he'd expected. Ethan was fairly certain hypnosis didn't work that easily and calculated it had more to do with the fact he actively intended to travel to the dream world.

Crisp autumn leaves crackled beneath his feet as he twisted around to make sure he was alone. The last thing he wanted was to run into that wolf again. Werewolf, he suspected. He had heard it speak before, so it was obviously not any standard species of wolf. He relaxed when he was sure nothing was surrounding him.

The night mirrored the one back home. The moon hung waxing and bright above him, lighting a dirt path into a wooded area. He had a strange sensation he'd been there before. Some faint memory tugging at him. No. Guiding him. He knew exactly where to go even though he wasn't sure why.

He followed the overgrown path through the trees. Time appeared to be passing differently. The stars above him zoomed past too quickly to be real; the world was spinning out of control. However, the earth he walked upon remained still. He arrived in a clearing after merely moments, but when he glanced over his shoulder, there was a dense forest behind him as if he'd traveled for hours.

"When you hear my voice say 'Come home, Ethan,' you will wake up. And when you tell yourself 'Go home, Ethan,' you will awaken." Grady's disembodied voice spoke to him through time and space. He was planting the anchor.

The experiment seemed to be going as planned, and Ethan found a surge of confidence. His sense of wonder and curiosity took control and he made his way to a crumbling stone shack set in the middle of the clearing. A peculiar place for anyone to build a structure, and it didn't seem anyone had visited it in quite some time.

As he approached the front, it became obvious that the structure had once been enclosed with metal bars that were now ripped open. This damage to the foundation was what had sent the small building into ruin.

"He escaped." A voice came from above, but this time it was not Grady's. The voice was female.

Startled, Ethan noticed a red fox perched on top of one of the remnants of a wall. Her cunning yellow eyes and amber fur shimmered in the moonlight. Ethan took a step back. Perhaps he should wake up now. It was probably the right thing to do. Instead, his inquisitive nature got the best of him.

"Who?" he asked the fox.

When the animal replied, its mouth did not move. It was communicating with him telepathically.

"You still don't know." He could have sworn it sounded disappointed in him.

Ethan's brow furrowed in confusion and he was at a loss for words.

"Marius," the fox finally clarified. "Marius is free. Somehow, he found the strength to free himself. I think someone may have helped him."

"Who is Marius?" Ethan glanced at the twisted metal bars and revised his question. "*What* is Marius?"

"A lycanthrope," she replied.

"So he *is* a werewolf. The one who keeps chasing me." Ethan scanned his surroundings once again with paranoia that he was being followed. Somewhere in the dense woods, he could sense eyes were watching him. An instinctual sense of unease set in.

"Yes," the fox confirmed.

"Who are you?" Ethan asked, but before she could answer, a voice summoned him.

"Come home, Ethan."

The ground was ripped out from under him, and his heart plummeted as if he were falling from a cliff. There was nothing but the abyss of space and stars floating all around him as he fell. Then his eyes flew open and he bolted upright on the bed.

Grady grabbed him by the shoulders to steady him. "Are you all right?"

Ethan nodded, catching his breath. "Yeah. I didn't expect it to be so...startling."

"Perhaps it will become easier the more you try it," Grady suggested. "However, I do not recommend purposefully attempting to go back. I'm only trying to give you the power to break free of that world should you ever end up in it. Your goal should be to escape that fate, not fall victim to it."

"Well, it worked." He sat with his legs crisscrossed and rubbed the sides of his arms to warm up. His body was inexplicably chilled. Slowly, he recollected the events that had transpired.

"There's something wrong there. It's unsafe."

His expression was a mix of bewilderment and concern.

"That's precisely why I *don't* want you to travel there on purpose. I know it might be tempting, but it's too dangerous."

"Marius," Ethan said as he remembered the name.

Grady's face grew pale. He pulled away from Ethan and stared so intently into his eyes Ethan wondered if he were trying to read his mind.

"That's the name of the wolf," Ethan explained. "The one from my dreams."

"You saw him again?"

"No. There was this fox. It told me his name."

Grady ran a hand through his hair as he attempted to make sense of Ethan's story. "A fox spoke to you?"

"It's hard to explain," Ethan finally said. "But, yeah, no worries. I don't want to go back. Not with that *thing* on the loose. I barely survived a vampire attack here, and that was only because I had you to save me. The last thing I want is to face a werewolf in a nightmare where I could actually die."

"You feel that way now, but there will be times when you'll want to go. The allure of it will be instinctual. It's part of who you are. You'll have to fight that temptation."

Ethan nodded his complete agreement.

Grady's tension eased. He glanced at his watch and then rubbed between his eyes to alleviate the stress that their experiment had brought on.

"It's late. And tomorrow will be exhausting for the both of us, I'm sure."

"Right," Ethan said as he remembered the coming Halloween party. Lots of monsters to entertain and keep in line. At least these were the kind who enjoyed parties and probably wouldn't attempt to murder him while socializing in Grady's home.

He slid off the bed, and Grady walked him to the door. Before he left, he turned and wrapped his arms around Grady, resting his head against the other man's chest.

Grady reciprocated the embrace, squeezing him tightly with one arm and grasping the back of his neck with the other in a manner Ethan read as longing.

"Thank you," Ethan whispered.

"Whatever for?"

"For everything."

Ethan pulled away, giving him one last idolizing smile, and then left him alone.

ONCE ETHAN HAD gone, Grady exhaled audibly, realizing he'd been holding his breath, he supposed, in an effort to make the moment last.

This time, he was the one to fall onto his bed in defeat. This unexpected attraction to Ethan wasn't something he'd foreseen when he'd set this whole plan into motion. How could he have? It was years ago. And this was more than a fleeting attraction. He might actually be falling in love with him. Which was unsettling since he'd believed himself to be entirely incapable of ever loving anyone again. For two decades, the only passionate emotions he'd ever known were sorrow and hatred.

And now the final hour was drawing near. Halloween night. The full moon. A killing moon.

He had the key at his disposal. He had confirmation the wolf was indeed Marius. Everything had fallen into place perfectly.

Except that it wasn't perfect. He was conflicted. Everything was complicated in a completely different way than he'd predicted. It wasn't finding the Dream Traveler that was hard. Nor luring him into his home. Even separating him from his friends and family had been easier than expected. What had complicated everything was that the Dream Traveler wasn't some demon at all, as he'd imagined. He was a person. A real person with passions, hopes, and an entire life of endless potential ahead of him. And Grady had knowingly betrayed him even before he had ever met him.

He was a monster. He could never go through with it now. Not now that he knew this creature, who had once been nothing more than an abstract construct in his mind, was actually human. And someone he'd grown to care for. Deeply. Someone that he'd kissed and made promises to. And tomorrow, he was supposed to lead him to an almost certain death? He couldn't bear it.

He had little time to decide. Within twenty-four hours he would either put this all behind him and ignore it completely, or, he would finish the mission he'd started years ago. All of the work he had done building a life here, the research, the risks...they were all leading to this.

Once the house fell quiet enough he was certain everyone else had fallen asleep, Grady carefully closed his door and approached his armoire. He pulled out a minimally decorated antique wooden box that locked shut with a brass clasp. He took out his wallet and retrieved a small bronze skeleton key, setting the chest down on his dresser and unlocking it to reveal its contents. He hadn't gazed upon it in years. Not since he'd moved to Shady Pines.

His fingertips caressed the barrel of the aged pistol, bringing a flood of emotions. Rather, the memories of emotions past. Rage, sorrow, torment, and the vow of vengeance. They washed over him and his hand began to tremble. Illness overcame him. He had dedicated his entire life to this occasion. This brief moment in time where everything would align and he could finally execute his revenge.

Now he found himself questioning if he even wanted to. What would be the point? He'd changed drastically. He was a different man now than he was even a week before. But, there was an intoxicating attraction to giving in to his grief.

The familiar pain caused his hands to betray his heart. He reached into a compartment inside of the box, pulling out a silver bullet and loading it into the pistol. He placed the gun inside his nightstand drawer, where he'd always intended to plant it.

However, he had no intention of actually using it. He knew that now. But he carried out the ritual as a way to acknowledge how horrendous and cruel he'd become. He must always remember he would never be an acceptable match for Ethan. It would serve as a token of admonition to the selfish and twisted demons inside of him. The ones who had plotted to risk the very life of the one person he now cared for more than anyone or anything else.

He vowed to himself he would serve as his protector, though, for the rest of his life. This was his new mission. This was his answer. He would put all of this madness behind him.

He sat on the floor and leaned his head against the nightstand, closing his eyes with self-loathing.

Ethan's soul was gentle, kind, and pure. Knowing him had unlocked the realization his own soul had grown as dark and wicked as the demons he hated.

Fifteen: Stars in Your Eyes

EVERY TIME THE doorbell rang, Benny would scamper to the foyer, wagging his tail and barking excitedly. When the guests entered, he would then run in circles as if showing off the handiwork of his costume. Most arrivals took the time to compliment him on his choice, which would send his tail swishing even more vigorously.

The house was a lively din of noise considering most of its guests were dead, or undead. Music was playing loudly and all of the rooms on the bottom floor had been decorated with the flair of a gothic Venetian masquerade and opened up for everyone to mingle in freely.

Most of the prominent clients had already arrived and were either dancing, gossiping, or sticking their noses into corners around the house hoping to find out more about the enigmatic man who kept their existences hanging delicately under his pendulum of tolerance.

Wailing Walter, the overly dramatic banshee, had carefully positioned himself near the dessert table so he had plenty of opportunities to share his gloom with anyone who wasn't already wise enough to avoid him.

A gaggle of female ghosts congregated in the hallway in an effort to be the first to see everyone as they arrived and then gossip about them as soon as they made their way into the study; which had quickly become the prime residence of the bulk of the party as everyone agreed the room was far more massive and intriguingly superior to any of the other areas downstairs.

Grady, dressed as the Phantom of the Opera, made an elegant welcome to everyone as they arrived. It was tradition for him to greet all of his guests personally before finally joining them in the midst of the party.

His attention this Halloween, however, kept diverting to the staircase as he waited for Ethan to finally make an appearance. The party had begun promptly at nine o'clock and now it was nearly half an hour later and the young man still hadn't come down to join them. He worried maybe something was wrong or Ethan was even more timid than he'd realized.

The doorbell rang for what must have been the hundredth time, and Grady plastered on the same charming smile he welcomed everyone with as he opened the door.

"Vivian! So good to see you! Thomas." He beamed and greeted her boyfriend, avoiding direct eye contact and let them both in.

"I've been eager to ask how things went last night." He also offered compliments on their costumes. Vivian was dressed as a flapper girl in a sparkling white dress, and Thomas complimented her with a matching suit.

Grady smiled. "How very Gatsby of you."

"Well, it looks like the party is at your place tonight," Thomas conceded in an effort to be cordial.

"Oh, last night." Vivian scanned the crowd like she had someone in particular she was searching for. "It was fine."

"Really? Marguerite didn't give you any trouble?" Grady inquired. It seemed highly unlikely.

"Not at all. In fact, it was a waste of my time to even go over there." Vivian smiled pleasantly as she finally acknowledged him with her attention. She seemed as if she was trying to hide something, but Grady trusted her judgment and decided to let the matter go.

"That's a relief," Grady said. "Not a waste, though. Better to be cautious. Thank you for checking in on it for me."

"No problem." She grinned and then led Thomas into the party without another glance in Grady's direction. *Probably for the best.* He enjoyed Vivian's company but wasn't particularly fond of having to be near Thomas longer than was necessary. Besides, the doorbell had declared another arrival.

When he opened the door, he was greeted by two dapper gentlemen in Victorian-era suits and top hats. Both had goggles attached to their hats, but one was dressed in shades of cerulean and navy blue. The other in shades of crimson and garnet that complemented his well-groomed raven hair and made one think of a fine red wine or a gothic romance with too much bloodshed.

"Lover! I haven't heard a peep from you in so long! I was telling Marcus here I hoped you hadn't gone and died before the party. What a shame that would've been!" the stunning dandy in red declared. It was Dacey Sinnett and he glided into the house as if he were as welcome as ever.

"Still entirely alive. I try not to disappoint," Grady responded. For the first time since he'd known him, he was ashamed to even be in the same proximity with Dacey, let alone hearing him call him his lover. He was sure he had visibly cringed but thankfully his mask blocked a full view of his face and Dacey didn't seem to notice.

"I'm afraid you'll have to invite Marcus in," Dacey reminded him politely. "Silly vampire rules, you know."

"Oh, yes. Please, come in, Marcus."

Marcus was as youthful and attractive as Dacey. Beneath his hat, blond curls peeked out and his eyes were vibrant amber. His face was naturally chiseled in a way that gave him an air of nobility but his cool demeanor conveyed complete apathy. Grady thought they made a stunning pair.

"I don't think I've had the pleasure," Grady said, extending a hand in greeting to Marcus. Marcus glanced down at the gesture and hesitated but eventually shook his hand briefly as a sneer fluttered across his lips.

"Marcus is my sire," Dacey explained. "He arrived in town yesterday, passing through on his way to some tedious reunion somewhere, and he couldn't resist dropping in to say hello."

Dacey reached over to tuck a wild curl of hair into the other vampire's hat.

"He's always so worried about me when really I'm the one who is always watching out for him," he added affectionately.

"Well, it's nice to finally meet you." Grady said to Marcus, who continued to stare coolly at him without speaking. Grady couldn't help but wonder if Marcus might be a clue in deciphering their current vampire problem, but he seemed so standoffish he wasn't sure how to ask.

Dacey swooped over to stand beside Grady. "I've told him all about you," he said, and then whispered hotly into his ear. "I don't think he approves, but maybe if we let him watch then he'll see the appeal."

Grady's cheeks burned, and he cleared his throat as he took a step away from the lustful vampire, grasping desperately for something to say to distract him.

"I...love your suits. You're both very dashing," Grady finally managed.

"Oh, these old things?" Dacey laughed and rolled his eyes. "Please. We've literally had them for a century. Added the goggles, though, as they seem to be in vogue amongst the creatives these days. I always do enjoy a good subcultural trend. Although, Marcus made the valid point that they are extremely frivolous.”

“Well, what’s the point in wearing a costume if you’re not going to be frivolous?”

“That’s exactly what I said!”

“Well, you two should go in and enjoy the party. I’ll be in shortly.” Grady hoped to get Dacey ushered away before Ethan finally made his way down.

Dacey leaned in, whispering again. “I was hoping maybe we could steal away together later, like we did two years ago behind the garden. Under the full moon. How ravishing would that be?”

It was too hot under Grady’s mask, so he took it off and pulled it onto his right bicep allowing the elastic to hold it into place like an armband.

“We need to talk,” he whispered. “I can’t do this anymore.”

Dacey seemed puzzled. Marcus, clearly able to hear all of the whispering without any trouble, rolled his eyes.

“What? Why ever not?” Dacey pried.

He quickly got his answer as Grady opened his mouth to respond but was immediately distracted by a figure descending the staircase nearby. Dacey stole a glance and then a mischievous grin engulfed him and he chuckled.

“It’s as I feared then,” Dacey said, feigning sorrow. “I’ve lost you to the virgin saint. Or is he sans virginity now? I can’t keep up with your relationships. They move too fast.”

“Stop,” Grady warned, wishing the two vampires would leave him alone. He noticed Ethan seemed to be examining their body language as he approached, which wasn’t comforting to Grady since Dacey was still practically hanging all over him.

"Ethan Roam! I've so been looking forward to seeing your resplendent visage again," Dacey shouted, throwing his arms around him and kissing him on the cheek like they were old friends.

Ethan's eyes widened in confusion, fear, and possibly arousal. Dacey had that effect on practically everyone whether they wanted him to or not.

"Hey." Ethan nodded a greeting to Marcus, but he only replied by squinting at him in distaste.

"That's Marcus," Grady informed Ethan flatly. He scanned his appearance. He was wearing a red-and-black striped sweater, black pants, and a brown hat.

"Where's your costume?"

Ethan grinned and revealed the hand he'd been hiding behind his back. He had a brown glove with knifed fingers he wiggled at Grady's face.

"This *is* my costume. I'm Freddy Krueger," he explained, entirely too pleased with himself.

Grady laughed. "Dream demon? You have a twisted sense of humor."

"Thank ya," Ethan said with a grin. "Anyway, sorry it took me so long to get down here. I was going to do all the face makeup, but then I was like, blah, that sounds like too much work."

Dacey strolled confidently behind Ethan and wrapped his arms flirtatiously around his shoulders. "It's for the best, love. We wouldn't want you messing up that dazzling face of yours, anyway."

Ethan cast a pleading gaze to Grady for help, but Grady just shrugged as the doorbell rang again. There was really only one guest unaccounted for and that meant this had to be Arthur.

Grady opened the door wide, expecting to see the portly older gentleman standing there, but was instead captivated by an angelically stunning female face. Her auburn hair cascaded in smooth waves down her shoulders, her pouted lips were painted a muted pink that complemented her nearly porcelain-like skin, and she had familiar doe eyes like two blue pools that would easily serve as portals to some version of heaven. Those were the thoughts that flew through Grady's mind as this stranger, this beautiful woman in medieval period dress, stood at his door and stared at him for a moment as if casting instantaneous judgment upon him. Grady then noticed standing directly behind this siren of the night was, indeed, Arthur—dressed as King Arthur—and he was wearing a smug expression as if it were the best accessory.

Ethan quickly pulled himself out from Dacey's embrace and moved for the door. "Mom? What are you doing here?"

Everything inside of Grady shattered as reality finally confronted him.

"Please, come in," Grady offered, reluctantly welcoming Ethan's mother and Arthur into the house. As he shut the door behind them, he covertly grabbed Arthur by the elbow and leaned in where only he could hear.

"What are you up to?" he asked through clenched teeth as he feigned a smile.

"What? I'm not allowed a plus one?" Arthur brushed him off, moving forward to stand with the beautiful woman who was hugging Ethan.

Dacey and Marcus, disinterested in the new arrivals, hastily left the foyer and joined the rest of the party. No doubt Dacey wanted to gather as much gossip as he could now that everyone was together.

"I'm so glad you're all right. I've been so worried!" Ethan's mother said as she pulled back from their greeting.

Ethan rushed to apologize. "I know. I'm sorry. I got really...busy."

She eyed him with criticism. "Too busy to even send a text? And what's this about you moving out of your apartment? You live *here* now?"

She examined her surroundings and thankfully seemed more pleasantly surprised than judgmental. Grady still cast Arthur a sideways glance of displeasure with his obvious meddling and the professor hastily made an attempt to satisfy everyone.

"I'm sorry but I felt stuck in the middle. You're all my friends," he expressed earnestly. "Your mother has been a nervous wreck, even though I told her I knew you were fine, and so I thought what better way to fix the situation than to get us all together in one place?"

"Yes. A truly fantastic estimation," Grady agreed sarcastically.

"Karen, this is Doctor Grady Hunter." Arthur, ignoring Grady's sour disposition, formally introduced them. "And Grady, this is Karen Roam."

Grady, ever the charming host, put his dissatisfaction aside and produced a charismatic smile as he took Karen's hand and rose it to his lips giving her delicate skin a polite kiss. He noted her hand was as smooth as velvet and smelled of lavender.

"It's a pleasure to finally meet you, Ms. Roam. You're certainly a stunning woman," Grady said, purposefully making eye contact with her and letting his gaze give the impression he was mesmerized with her beauty. It wasn't a task to produce the charm at all as he actually did find her quite attractive. His attempt at winning her over seemed to produce a positive effect as she gave a nervous laugh.

"Well, thank you." She smiled, her concerned face had suddenly become one of youthful delight. "You're very striking yourself, Doctor Hunter."

Ethan cleared his throat to remind them he was standing there. Unfortunately, his call for attention seemed to remind Karen of a rehearsed inquisition she'd prepared before arriving.

"How long have you known my son?" she asked Grady pointedly. He knew she was baiting him. The wrong response would send this confrontation into a sour direction and he could see in her eyes *any* response would probably be the wrong one.

"*Mom,*" Ethan intervened, his tone laced with embarrassment.

"*Ethan,*" she responded sternly. She continued, interrogating Grady, "You're much older than he is. Nearer my age? I'm sure you can see the red flags. So please, enlighten me on how my son came to drop everything in his life and move in with you, without so much as a second thought on informing his own mother? You know I was paying his rent, right? So now, I guess you're the one footing the bill?"

Grady couldn't get a word in edgewise.

"I mean, look at this place! This is ridiculous," she went on. "I'm starting to wonder which of you is the one manipulating the other..."

She scrutinized them both accusingly. Arthur, hovering nearby, seemed to be enjoying the admonishment.

"There are no manipulations, I assure you," Grady insisted respectfully. "Ethan and I genuinely have each other's best interests in mind. To be blunt, Ms. Roam, I feel it's a blessing he came into my life and I hope that he feels the same."

"I do." Ethan smiled fondly at him. Grady was thankful for his testimony. "I'm really sorry I didn't tell you, but this is exactly why. You worry *so* much. But look! I'm totally fine. And I'm happy. In fact, I haven't even had one of my nightmares since I met Grady."

Of course he was embellishing, as he most certainly had, but this revelation seemed to be all she needed to back down. Her loving gaze met her son's and a tender expression consumed her features.

"That's wonderful," she said.

Grady noticed cheerful tears were welling up in her eyes and he valiantly produced his handkerchief to her.

"Thank you." She nodded to him approvingly. "I must seem silly but you have to understand he's struggled for so long with his...problems. It's hard to believe they've stopped, but if your influence is the reason then perhaps...I should give you a fair chance."

"That would be an incredible kindness." Grady beamed at her as she passed his handkerchief to him. "You seem to be an incredible mother and you've raised...Well, the best man I've ever had the pleasure to know. I look forward to getting to know you better as well."

"Sorry to crash your party," she said, flustered.

"You did no such thing," Grady said. "In fact, you've made it ten times better as you're clearly the belle of the ball. All the men will be very delighted to have you here as soon as they lay eyes on you."

She gave another charmed giggle and then teased Ethan, "I can see why you've been distracted."

Grady stood up straighter with self-satisfaction. Now that their confrontation had resolved, he began to usher everyone into the study where most of the party's activity was taking place.

As they walked, Arthur held out a small package to Ethan who took it curiously.

"I thought it would be nice to bring you a sort of housewarming gift," he explained.

"Thanks." Ethan grinned, opening the package. "It's one of your books? I don't think I've ever heard of this one before."

"It's one of my lesser known works." Arthur produced a mischievous smile and shrugged. "I thought you might find some interesting ideas in there. I even highlighted a few of my favorite parts."

Grady, listening in to the conversation happening behind him, stole a glance at the book in Ethan's hands. It was a copy of *The Mechanics of Sleep Travel*. Fear and desperation consuming him, he whirled around and swiped the book out of Ethan's grasp. It was such a sudden expression of panic, they all paused to stare at him suspiciously. Well, except for Karen, who was too busy being dumbfounded by the sight of ghosts gliding in and out of rooms. It was a good thing she wasn't the fainting type as none of the men would have been paying enough attention to catch her.

"How nice of you, Arthur," Grady pretended to thank him. "I'll add this to the bookshelf and Ethan can flip through it later."

"He could take it to his room if he'd like. With his other belongings," Arthur countered, eying Grady distrustfully.

"Nonsense! My belongings are his belongings. It's his home now too. I'll go put this up."

"But you already have your own copy," Arthur argued, knowingly revealing information he had suspected Grady hadn't confessed.

"No, you must be mistaken," Grady insisted emphatically. "I do have a lot of your books but not this one."

"But—" Arthur was about to call him out but Ethan intervened, not understanding what the big fuss was between the two older men.

"It's okay. It can go in the bookshelf. I really don't mind." He took the book from Grady and carried it over to the shelf himself and placed it within.

THE PARTY CONTINUED on around them even with Grady and Arthur locked in a mutual glare. Karen had been distracted by Benny who had brought over his favorite squeaky bone for a game of tug-of-war.

"What an adorable little dog," she said. Benny wagged his tail with pride.

"He's something else, that's for sure."

Ethan caught sight of Vivian and Thomas near the dessert table and waved in greeting at them. Thomas was, unfortunately, the latest victim of one of Wailing Walter's gloomy stories. Ethan was about to make his way over to save him when Dacey seemed to appear out of nowhere before him.

"Ethan! We saw the painting of you! Marcus simply *adores* it. I must buy it for him. Do you think Grady would be willing to give it up?" he asked, interlocking their arms together and forcing Ethan into a stroll over toward the antique piano where a canvas sat facing the wall, still on its easel. It was the one Grady had painted the night after the vampire fight.

Ethan hesitated. "I don't think that one is for sale." Ethan hesitated.

"Too bad! Although, I completely understand why you'd want to keep it. But now, I must ask you something very important." Dacey sounded serious. "And you must be honest with me now, no humble or meek replies..."

Dacey grabbed Ethan by his waist. He stared deep into his eyes; his own were piercing and flickered with passionate interest. "Do you really play the piano?"

"Yes," Ethan confirmed reluctantly. "I've been playing since I was a kid."

"He does play!" The stylish vampire's face lit up as he turned his gaze to Marcus, who was standing a couple of feet away, still admiring the painting. He didn't pay the two much attention but his expression gave the appearance this news pleased him.

"Does he ever talk?" Ethan asked.

"Only when it's of great importance. Otherwise, he feels I do enough talking for the both of us," Dacey explained, before continuing.

"Marcus and I would love to hear you play something. We've always had a *thing* for musicians." Dacey produced a dazzlingly persuasive smile.

Ethan's cheeks heated. "I wouldn't want to disturb the party."

Dacey grabbed Ethan's mouth firmly in one hand and chided him, "I said no meek replies. Besides, live music is crucial for any worthwhile party."

Marcus administered an imperial nod of accord to Dacey's statement.

Then, like an excited child, Dacey grabbed Ethan by the hands and batted his eyelashes as he begged, causing a glimpse of his fangs to show, *"Please!"*

Ethan couldn't help but give in. Even considering everything he now knew about the vampire, he still took delight in his attention.

"Fine.".

Dacey slipped a finger through one of Ethan's belt loops and pulled him in nearer, "I knew I'd win you over."

Ethan swore the temperature had suddenly risen ten degrees and the oversized sweater he wore only caused the sensation to amplify. He caught himself almost enticed by the vampire but then noticed Dacey steal a glance in Grady's direction and realized he was attempting to make his ex-lover jealous. However, Grady wasn't paying any attention to them. He was now caught up in a jovial conversation with Karen. Ethan seized the opportunity to be bold.

"You're very handsy," he said, pulling away from the vampire's grasp.

"Oh, I've been told I'm *very* good with my hands."

"Guess not good enough," Ethan countered smugly as he sat down at the piano. "Or else I wouldn't be the one caressing Grady's ivory, now would I? Musicians are really great with their hands." He took off his glove and slid his fingers gently over the keys to accentuate his quip.

He joined him on the piano bench, sitting intimately close to Ethan. "I'm afraid you have the wrong impression. It's not Grady I'm interested in. And I'm very familiar with the prowess of a musician's hands."

Dacey then played a small portion of the opening of Wilhelm Würfel's Fantaisie élégante, op. 45. If he was trying to impress Ethan, it worked—the vampire's skill took him by surprise.

Dacey leaned in and breathed a libidinous challenge.

"Your turn. Show me what you can do with *your* hands, Dreamer."

The nickname gave Ethan pause and a worrisome awareness crept into his mind. He glanced around to make sure no one was watching them. The only attention they had was that of Marcus, who had leaned against the end of the piano aloofly.

"Do you remember what you said to me when we met?" Ethan asked carefully, his voice hushed. Dacey's ears pricked at the indication a covert exchange was about to take place.

"Love, I say so many memorable things to so many people that, ironically, I forget all of them. I'm afraid you'll have to be more specific."

"You told me I have the stars in my eyes," Ethan reminded him. "How did you mean that, exactly?"

Dacey's own eyes lit up with fancy. "Oh yes! Well, I admit it wasn't merely a compliment but rather...an observation."

This was all the confirmation Ethan needed.

"So...you know?" He leaned in closer. At this point they were so intimately close in conversation that the tips of their noses were practically touching.

"You know what I am?" Ethan inquired more specifically.

Dacey rested his hand on Ethan's knee.

"Darling heart, of course I do. I know everything about everyone. It's kind of my thing."

Ethan's mouth dropped open. "How?"

"Those are *my* secrets," Dacey answered vaguely, pulling away.

"You can never tell anyone," Ethan demanded of him. "Not ever. I'm serious."

"My lips will not betray you," Dacey promised.

Ethan glowered at him. "I hope not.".

"Look at us!" Dacey laughed, brushing off the sober tone of the conversation. "We're practically best friends now. Sharing secrets at parties. You do consider me a friend, I hope?"

Ethan weighed the idea and then answered strictly, "If you can keep quiet about me and keep your hands off of Grady, then yes. We can be friends."

"Duly noted...that you *didn't* specify that I had to keep my hands off of *you.*"

Ethan smiled noncommittally. He glanced over at Grady, who was still with his mother. He had his hand placed on the small of her back as he guided her in a tour of the room pointing to different paintings as they carried on some discussion. They were also sharing a few laughs.

"Your mother must be quite the conversationalist," Dacey remarked.

"Yeah. I don't know what's going on with all that," he said irksomely. "I mean, I want them to like each other but they almost seem to like each other too much. It's kind of weirding me out."

"That's Grady for you. He's a notorious heart breaker, sorry to say. Though it's never purposeful on his part. He can't help it if others choose to make fools of themselves over him. I actually find him quite refreshing. Most humans are rather disenchanting company but Grady...well, he's something exceptional, isn't he?"

"Did you love him?" Ethan had already heard Grady's side of the story but the more he talked to Dacey, the more he wondered if Grady had been embellishing. The vampire actually seemed very amiable. It was hard to imagine there wasn't more between them than physical attraction.

"Time is wasted dwelling on past matters of the heart. I think the real question is, do *you* love him?"

Ethan couldn't meet Dacey's eyes. The answer he had to provide was too real, too personal to acknowledge sharing with anyone. Love was something so foreign and new to him he had been intoxicating himself with it by keeping it a close secret. Up until this point, he hadn't uttered the truth aloud.

He played a few notes on the piano and faintly replied, "Yes."

If it were anyone else, they probably wouldn't have even caught his response over the din of the party but words were never lost around a vampire.

"Does he know?"

Ethan wasn't sure how to answer. He'd never said it but shouldn't Grady be able to pick up on all the obvious signs? *Did* he know? He thought so, but it had also never been acknowledged.

"You should tell him," Dacey advised sweetly. "I think it would do him well to know someone loves him."

Ethan smiled gratefully at Dacey. There was definitely more to the vampire than he let on. At the surface he was lusty and raucous but inside there was someone full of wisdom and, Ethan wondered, possibly compassion? Not entirely the deviant beast Grady had made him out to be. Then again, Ethan reasoned with mild skepticism, it could be possible Dacey was a social chameleon who was whomever he needed to be for whomever he was with.

"Now, play me a song *I* can fall in love to." Dacey stood to take up company next to Marcus, who at this point seemed to have lost all interest in anything at the party and was busy texting on his phone.

"I think I know just the one." Ethan began to play. It was an old song he'd heard many times when he was young—"Stars in Your Eyes", a lesser-known Sinatra tune his mother used to play on sad days when she was missing his father. Dacey's remark the other day had recalled the memory of it and he had since been humming it to himself and working out the notes in his mind. He had to wonder, had the song been special to his parents because someone once paid his father the same compliment the vampire had given him?

As a child, he hadn't known the song to mean anything sad. It always sounded like what it was intended to be—a sentimental love song. As he grew older, he realized his mother only played it when she was sad. Eventually, a day came where she didn't play it at all. To Ethan, it had only been a nostalgic song from his childhood. He didn't associate it to the father who had died so mysteriously. They'd been told he'd suffered from a heart attack while he was away on business. Now, Ethan wondered if it weren't something more sinister. But none of that affected the memory of the melody. For him, it was an expression of hope—a song that promised one day he too could experience the depth of the lyrics toward someone he'd fallen in love with.

Ethan had an excellent ear for music and easily found the rhythm. The song transitioned flawlessly from his memory to the keys and promptly caught the attention of the throng of guests. The next bit drew them in closer with rapt attention as he began to sing. Even Benny quieted down long enough to listen.

It was the first time any of them had heard him sing, with the exception of his mother and Arthur, and the crowd was immediately smitten. His vocals were a golden honey tenor and his performance was enhanced by the sincerity that emanated from his eyes and smile as he carried the tune along.

Besides Arthur, who had used the distraction to sneak off, the guests who were most familiar with Ethan had crowded around the piano. All eyes were on him as he performed but his only met one other pair as he sang. He had been performing his entire life and could easily block out the audience in his mind. For him, the only audience he had or wanted was Grady. And Grady appeared completely enraptured in the gesture.

His voice lilted with a sweet intonation as he hit the last note and the spellbound crowd applauded him. He gave a humble laugh and thanked them politely before they returned to socializing and sharing their thoughts on how talented Grady's new apprentice was. It was safe to say he'd earned a few new fans.

Dacey hugged Ethan tightly and thanked him for the performance. Even Marcus made the effort to shake his hand and shower him with adulation. But, all that Ethan could pay any attention to was Grady standing across from him at the end of the piano. He wondered why he seemed so somber as the man simply offered him a bittersweet smile.

His mom joined him on the piano bench once everyone had milled away. "So, you're really happy here?" she asked. Grady was still hanging around but he was in a deep conversation with Dacey who had left Marcus to his own devices since he was, once again, more interested in the text conversation he had been having than anything going on at the party.

"Very," Ethan happily insisted.

"Good. Don't forget to keep in touch from now on. Okay?" she reiterated. Ethan hugged his mom to assure her he would.

"I have one more question for you, though," she said as she pulled away. Ethan glanced at her quizzically.

"How did he set up the ghosts?" she asked with amazement. "They're not repeating any patterns. Is it a very long loop? Are they being projected from somewhere? I can't seem to figure it out, but it's a really great effect!"

Ethan laughed heartily as he struggled to decide if he should break the news to her they weren't Halloween decorations.

Sixteen: The Killing Moon

THE PARTY CONTINUED, but Grady felt miles away. Although Ethan's song had ended, it still held Grady in its grip. There are those defining moments in life that push one to do or say things they never expected of themselves. To feel things they never thought they could feel again. They will have thought they'd stalwartly decided on a path and then something, almost divine, takes place to swipe their conviction out from beneath them. Grady knew this song, this grand romantic gesture was that moment for him.

There would be no sweeping the past under the rug. There could be no more secrets. He had to set things right. He was compelled to confess his ultimate sins. He couldn't proposition Ethan to carry on a lifetime with him based on lies. That seemed as decisively cruel as the scheme he'd concocted in the first place to entice him into, what could have been, almost certain death. He had to come clean and give Ethan the chance to make up his own mind about their future together once he knew the truth. Even if that meant risking losing him forever.

Grady tensed as Dacey approached him. Although, he did notice he was careful not to stand too closely this time.

"Well, I suppose if I had to lose you to anyone then at least it was Ethan as he's obviously the only acceptable choice," Dacey teased.

"Thanks for your well-wishes?" Grady wasn't really sure how to respond to such a statement. He eyed the vampire analytically. "It really doesn't upset you? You're fine with it?"

"Of course it upsets me!" Dacey said in mock offense. "I've lost the best part of my afternoons."

"That's all you're upset about?" Grady asked again. He wanted to make sure there would be no sour notes between them. The last thing he needed at the moment was a scorned vampire plotting revenge.

"I would be a fool to think you'd want anything to do with me when you've got a demigod fawning over you."

"Wait—you know? How much?"

"All of it. That he's a Dream Traveler, has psychic powers, can travel to other worlds if he wants. There are even legends that purport they can travel through time, did you know that? It's never been verified, though," Dacey responded excitedly. "I knew what he was from the moment I peered into his eyes like a scrying ball. There are perks to being a telepathic vampire, you know. Plus, the introduction gave it away. Not too many Shady Pines residents sporting the surname of Roam. And he really does resemble Vincent. Shorter in stature but you can definitely see it in his features."

Grady was taken aback. "You knew his father? Why didn't you say anything?"

"It didn't seem pertinent," Dacey answered flatly.

Grady frowned. "Your remarks are rarely pertinent."

"Fine. I like having my secrets and I was curious to know him better," Dacey admitted. "If I'd told you from the start you would have whisked the adorable little deity away from me and I never would have gotten the chance to read him properly."

"He's not a god," Grady corrected.

"He's closer to one than any other being on this planet, and he doesn't even know it. But you do. You haven't told him. I've read you both now. He has no idea of *everything* he's capable of."

"He will," Grady sighed.

"Good!" Dacey seemed relieved. "He's madly in love with you, you know. Please excuse me for being the one to put that out there. I know he should tell you himself but I'm not sure he has the courage to do it yet and you really should know. Especially if you've been keeping dire secrets from him. There's nothing more damning in a relationship than a secret kept by a lover for far too long. Not to mention, the longer he goes without knowing, the more danger he's in. If you don't tell him then someone else will and it could be exposed to his detriment...and possibly, everyone else's as well."

"Is that a threat?" Grady asked. Dacey's words had stabbed at his guilt in all the right places and the expression of assumed confrontation must have read clearly across his features.

"It's a plea," Dacey clarified. "As your friend, I'm vehemently requesting you reveal the truth to him. Do it soon. Before he becomes fearless and gives you his heart entirely."

"Is that what you think we are? Friends?" Grady's cutting inquiry was the first thing said that night that actually seemed to resonate with the vampire. His eyes echoed empty.

"Are we not?" he demanded softly. Grady remained silent.

"Well, I'm not going to pretend that doesn't sting. All of this time? Everything we shared? You didn't even view me as a friend? I find that hard to believe." He made an effort to read Grady's eyes but Grady diverted his gaze to block him.

"I knew it." Dacey seemed triumphant. "You wouldn't look away if you didn't have something to hide. You did care."

"Don't be ridiculous. I would've just as soon killed you if I had to. I still would."

"It would be a crime of passion then," Dacey teased. "No hard feelings, lover. You can't break my heart. It stopped beating a long time ago."

Such a sentiment from a vampire made Grady lose his grip on the last bit of cruelty he had locked inside of him. If this monster had truly believed they were friends and was able to forgive his horrible treatment of him, then how could he possibly justify any of his abhorrent actions? Remorseful, he realized he'd used Dacey as a means to a toxic addiction and, tragically, the entire time the vampire thought they were sharing an intimate connection. Grady's antipathy for himself pushed him over the edge. He used to think he was a man fighting monsters, but now it was discernibly clear he was a monster fighting with himself.

"I'm so sorry," Grady said. "For everything."

"You and I now seek the same thing. Redemption."

"I doubt I can ever earn that."

"Try," Dacey commanded. "Start tonight. Tell Ethan. Tell him everything."

Grady accepted the challenge, as he'd already decided to tell Ethan anyway, and gave Dacey an earnest embrace. A hug that expressed the new truth of their solidarity.

Dacey smiled sweetly and whispered, "Now, go. Show that boy he can conquer worlds...before the world conquers him. Besides, I have to bid adieu to Marcus. He's eager to meet up with some of our old friends in Dallas."

"What would a bunch of vampires be doing in Dallas?" Grady asked, almost foolishly.

"Causing riots and getting blood drunk, I'm sure," Dacey answered. Grady was affronted and immediately glared at Marcus from afar.

"I'm afraid you can't save the world all at once," Dacey said. "And I can't allow you to harm Marcus. Literally, I'm bound to protect him as he's my sire. I would hate to be at odds with you like that now I've *finally* earned your friendship. Know I haven't shared his lack of moral viewpoints for many decades. There's a reason we no longer live together."

"Do me a favor, will you? If Marcus or any other of your old vampire friends show up in Shady Pines again anytime soon, please let me know immediately."

"I certainly will. In all honesty, it wouldn't be my preference for any of them to ever set foot here. I make an exception for my sire, however. He's always proven irresistible to me; even before I became a vampire," Dacey explained.

Ethan had finally found his moment to approach Grady as his mother had wandered off to mingle with all the guests who fascinated her. Dacey pulled away from Grady quickly as he walked over to them.

"It was completely platonic touching, I promise," he insisted, holding up his hands in his defense. "Absolutely no one was aroused."

Ethan crinkled his nose. "Okay." He glanced to Grady and raised his eyebrows hopefully. "Want to step out for a minute?"

"It's happening," Dacey whispered to Grady through clenched teeth, not at all achieving whatever level of inconspicuousness he was hoping for. Grady shushed him and quickly parted away from the vampire's company.

"I was about to ask you the same thing," Grady responded to Ethan. "Let's go upstairs, I think we need to talk."

"We do indeed," Arthur interjected, strolling up to them with determination written all over his face. He had been so distracted it was only at that moment when Grady finally realized he had been missing from the group for quite some time.

"I don't know what you're playing at here, Grady, but the other copy of that book is missing. I know you had it in your collection before," Arthur accused angrily.

"I told you, I never owned a copy of that book," Grady said, attempting to make the other man seem foolish. "I don't see why it's such a controversy. I'll simply read Ethan's copy later if it means that much to you."

"I knew it!" Arthur declared. "Damn you, Hunter! How could you do this to me?"

Grady politely excused himself from Ethan's company and pulled Arthur to the side.

"Keep it together! You're drawing too much attention."

"What are you hiding? Why haven't you told him?" Arthur demanded. "I swear to God, Grady. If anything happens to him, I'll be the one hunting you."

"I was waiting for the right time. Which is now. Please, give me tonight to deal with this." Grady rested his palms on either of the other man's shoulders to try to placate him.

"Fine. But if he doesn't know the truth by tomorrow then I'm going to be the one to tell him," Arthur countered, finally lowering his voice.

"Of course. Thank you, my friend." Grady nodded appreciatively. He then returned to Ethan, who had been silently gawking at the two in an attempt to deduce what was going on.

"What was that about?" Ethan wondered.

"Too much to drink, I'm afraid," Grady lied. "Arthur's always been a lightweight."

Grady took Ethan by the hand affectionately in order to distract him from any further questions on the subject. Ethan was easily diverted by this gesture and the two left the party and made their way upstairs to the much more quiet and intimate setting of Grady's room.

As soon as he shut the door behind him, Grady turned around to begin the arduous task of confessing the horrible truth but was caught off guard by Ethan's overly amorous actions.

Ethan pulled him in tight and kissed him so passionately that, for a brief moment, Grady forgot there was a dark cloud looming over their future. Ethan's lips were lush and velvety and Grady was consumed with desire as their tongues met for the first time. He wanted nothing more than to ignore the reality of the situation and give in to his temptations. He could tell Ethan afterward.

"Wait." Grady halted. How could he have even had such a selfish thought, knowing he'd come to confess all the other selfish acts he'd already committed against him? He couldn't abuse Ethan's faith in him any more than he already had.

Ethan didn't seem to realize Grady was experiencing any form of conflict and persisted. "I have to tell you something. It's the most important thing I've ever said to anyone."

"Before you do, please, let me tell you something first."

"No, I have to do it now before I lose my courage," Ethan went on. "Grady, I l—"

"I lied to you," Grady interrupted.

Ethan stopped midsentence, blinking in confusion

"About what?" he finally asked.

"I owned that stupid book," was all Grady could gather the bravery to respond with.

"Arthur's book?" Ethan furrowed his brow. "Okay. I don't really care about a dumb book. I really need to talk to you about something important."

"I burned it because I didn't want you to find it. I didn't want you to know its secrets." Grady's bumbling confession continued. He leaned against the door as he spoke to keep Ethan from exiting the moment he would finally grow angry.

"Please, sit down," he instructed with distress, gesturing to the bed. Obviously caught off guard, Ethan did as instructed, growing silent to listen to Grady's revelation.

Grady breathed a deep breath to steady himself and find his resolve to do the right thing. It was exceedingly hard with Ethan staring at him tensely with his angelic eyes. He seemed so virtuous and clean Grady regretted he would have to rip away some of that innocence with the cruel truth of life. The truth of betrayal.

"You can do so much more than just travel in dreams, Ethan." He finally moved away from the door and went to sit in the chair near his desk as he wasn't sure how long this conversation would last. He was afraid if he stayed standing he would be consumed in his habit of pacing.

"Yeah, we already talked about that," Ethan argued.

"No, not just what happened in the cemetery," Grady said. "Although, there's more to that as well. Those talents are accentuated by emotion. The more emotional you are the more they manifest. That's the reason why I told you to learn to control your emotions better."

"Oh," Ethan said reluctantly.

"There's also the matter of memory manipulation and the ability to bend the laws of physics. Which is all very small in the grand scheme of things. Those who know of your kind believe you are the key to the universe. The dream world is the entry point to access an infinite system of multiverses. In simple terms, you have the inherent ability to travel to other worlds and dimensions by astral projection."

"Wh-what?" Shocked didn't even begin to describe the expression on Ethan's face.

"I know it's a lot to accept," Grady said. "The more you utilize your abilities the stronger they will grow. There are those who would seek to use you for nefarious purposes. They have done this in the past; to your ancestors. These creatures have enslaved your kind before and forced you to take them across the dimensional gates in order to further their own conquests. How do you think supernatural beings made it to Earth in the first place? It's why humans are so unequipped to deal with them. They weren't meant to be here. That's why I hadn't told you and why I'd insisted you not exercise your abilities. I never wanted anything like that to happen to you."

"This is all in that book?" Ethan asked. "So, Arthur knew too?"

"Yes," Grady said. "But, the book was actually written by your father, Vincent Roam. He had it published in an effort to try to find others who might be like him. Although, I don't know why as clearly he was the last of his line, until your mother had you, of course. Perhaps it was wishful thinking or a subconscious act of leaving behind his legacy."

"Or making sure I'd find out the truth one day if I were ever separated from him."

"I hadn't considered that," Grady admitted.

"Okay, well, all this overprotection from you and Arthur is really annoying," Ethan said. "I mean, think of how much further along I'd be if you guys had told me all of this from the beginning."

"Yes, but the point was I didn't want you to be further along. And Arthur wanted you to be safe."

"So why tell me now?" Ethan finally asked the question Grady was dreading to have to answer most. He would finally get to tell Ethan how he felt but in the most lamentable way.

"Because I fell in love with you," Grady answered miserably. "And I hadn't calculated for that. Ethan, you will surely hate me for this but you must know it now... I've been hunting you down for practically your entire life. And before I fell in love with you, there was a very real possibility I might have let you die tonight."

"This is insane," Ethan said as though he didn't want to believe any of it.

Grady wished he *were* lying. "It was insane," Grady agreed. "It terrifies me thinking about what I almost allowed to happen. What I almost *caused* to happen. I haven't been in my right mind for many years but you've snapped me back."

"What do you mean you were hunting me?" Ethan pressed, clearly torn. "Like a monster? You wanted to *kill* me?"

"No!" Grady quickly clarified. "I didn't want to kill you. I wanted to use you... Which, isn't really much better."

"Use me." Ethan spat the words at him as though they made him sick, "For what purpose? To travel to another world, like the creatures you talked about? To enslave me? Why would you want to do that?"

Grady exhaled heavily with grief. There were no acceptable justifications for his actions. Ethan would never be able to understand his motives, and who could blame him? Grady didn't even understand them fully anymore.

"When I was attempting to find a means of contacting Ava's spirit, I wound up in Romania," Grady began. "I had been told one of the most powerful mediums in the world, Madame Doru, was there and after months of searching, I finally found her in Targu Mures. She was an intense woman, elderly, and not very kind but she took an interest in my story. I witnessed her do incredible things and she had no interest in my money; she actually wanted to help me. We tried a few unsuccessful endeavors to reach Ava and then something entirely unexpected occurred. I had let her into my mind so she could see my memory of that horrible night. She believed this would help her in connecting with the right spirit. Instead, it connected her to something else. She had a vision of the wolf. Ava's spirit didn't read in her psychic scope, but she was able to pick up on the wolf's. She told me he had a name. Marius."

"The wolf from my dream," Ethan said, and then corrected himself. "The Dream World."

Grady nodded. "Yes. And that's precisely the message she conveyed to me. Marius was still alive but he existed outside of consciousness. Something had imprisoned him in an alternate existence. Madame Doru advised I would never be able to contact Ava. Her spirit had moved to another plane that is unreachable. However, Marius...there was the very real possibility I could find him. That I could seek out vengeance if I found the creature who could take me to this foreign realm."

"Me," Ethan said.

"The *Somnium Viator*," Grady confirmed. "And so began my hunt. That inkling of hope. That feeble idea of a connection to the past put a spark in me. That there was some chance I could seek out my revenge against the demon who killed Ava; this became the fire that fueled me... The fire almost died out. For a couple of years after this revelation and much research, I had absolutely nothing to show in the way of progress. In fact, I'd found that the last *Somnium Viator* had already died and I began to lose all hope. Then several years ago, by pure luck, I ended up in a rundown bookshop in Prague. I had been called to the city to assist in an exorcism, which I performed quite regularly at that time because families were willing to pay a handsome fee and my travels and research frequently exhausted my pocketbook. I was actually on my way to the train station when the bookshop caught my eye. I'm not entirely sure why I felt motivated to go in but I did. I perused the shelves for quite some time because they had quite a fantastic collection of occult tomes and oddities. One in particular caught my eye as a lot of the books weren't English publications but this one was. *The Mechanics of Sleep Travel* by Dr. Arthur Ellis. Needless to say, I purchased the book and by the time my trek on the train was complete, I was full of determination to find the man who wrote it. Surely, he was a Dream Traveler."

Grady paused to survey Ethan. The young man was listening with intense curiosity but his expression conveyed the sad truth Grady had been expecting. There was no longer trust between them. Grady fought the lump forming in his throat and continued.

"Obviously, he was easy to track down," Grady went on. "So, within a few weeks' time, here I was. In Shady Pines. I quickly went to work establishing the whereabouts of all the local supernaturals, building up a name for myself, and creating a suitable facade to live within while putting my plan into motion. I contacted Arthur, befriended him, and you know the rest. Of course, I learned he wasn't the Dream Traveler, but I didn't press him on finding out who was or letting on I even knew what one was. It would've been too obvious so I waited, hoping to discover the information for myself while carrying on the guise of friendship. As it turns out, I didn't have to ask, he offered the information up one day. He knew what I did for a living here and was fascinated by it but also saw it as an opportunity to help lift a burden from his shoulders. He'd been given the task of protecting you. Your father had left it to him and he felt he wasn't entirely capable of living up to the role without help. Of course, I was beyond delighted to offer my services, but at the time he first mentioned you, you were only sixteen years old. I told him to wait and send you my way once you reached adulthood. The excuse I used for him was your abilities would remain dormant until you'd matured, which is true. However, my reasons were entirely selfish, I needed you to have no strings attached. You needed to be away from your mother, without curfews, school, all of those things that would have held you from devoting all of your time and allegiance toward me."

Grady stopped abruptly as hot tears wavered in the corners of his eyes. "How much do you hate me now? Should I even continue?"

Ethan's own had already started streaming silently down his cheeks a long time ago and he responded coldly, "A lot. And yes."

Grady's heart broke. Things would never be the same between them. Ethan would never gaze upon him admiringly as he had done shortly before. He would never bless his lips with the comforting presence of his own again. Grady wiped his tears away and forced himself to reveal the true depth of his own corruption.

"Everything timed out perfectly," Grady said, his voice wavering with the pain of self-inflicted sorrow. "I thought it wouldn't. It had been two years since you'd reached adulthood and Arthur hadn't mentioned it again. You were in college and beginning to make a life for yourself. I knew I needed to act soon because this year would be my best chance. You see, a full moon on Halloween night produces the optimum opportunity for a human, like myself, to be able to successfully travel across planes with you. The veil between worlds is already thin thanks to Samhain and supernatural powers are amplified, as you know, during a full moon. It's earned the nickname amongst the undead as the Killing Moon and it only happens once every nineteen years. I couldn't wait another two decades, so I called upon Arthur and insisted he send you over."

"This was your doing all along!" Ethan furiously wiped away a few tears. "Everything. From the very beginning. Every move was strategic! Everything you said to me. All the things we've experienced together. You were manipulating me."

Ethan's words were like arrows piercing his heart. How could he make him understand? "Not everything was planned. I didn't expect when I met you that you would be...well, *you*. I thought it would be like dealing with Dacey. I had no idea how human you would be. How optimistic, passionate, and kind you are. All of the things we've shared have been real. Those moments were all *real*."

"No, they weren't. Because I shared those things with a man who I thought was my friend. Someone who I thought I could trust. And now that man doesn't exist. I don't even know who you are!"

"Yes, you do! I *am* that man that you've known!" Grady said desperately. "The lie was in how we met. Not in what we became."

Ethan grew quiet in anguished contemplation.

"You've always been the better man," Grady added. "I never lied about that. Now you just know why. I was blind with hatred, with fear, with a senseless need for retribution. And at what cost? Bringing death to those who would care for me now? I was a fool! But I see that now. And I only hope one day you can forgive me for these trespasses against you."

"You were going to ask me to take you to the Dream World tonight, weren't you?" Ethan asked, appalled. .

"Yes," Grady admitted. "After the party. I was going to ask you to take me there and I was going to kill that beast and be done with this forever."

"And if I had refused?" Ethan asked carefully. "What then?"

Grady wished Ethan weren't so astute. "You were going to *force* me, weren't you?" Ethan accused. Grady remained silent which seemed to finally give life to the validity of the story and Ethan lost what little resolve he had left.

"How? How were you going to force me?" he demanded.

A pulse of fiery blue energy shot out from his body and knocked over every loose object in the room, causing the furniture to tremble, much like a small earthquake.

They both shared a moment of complete surprise at the event. Ethan was apparently too upset to be distracted for long, however, and he clenched his fists in an effort to contain what seemed to be another blowup building up inside of him.

"Ethan," Grady said in a soothing voice, holding up his hands in an attempt at peace as he tried to coax him into a calmer state.

"No," Ethan snapped. "Stop! You don't get to say my name anymore. Not like that. Now answer the question!"

Grady bowed his head in shame. "I was going to hypnotize you."

It was as though his words had slapped Ethan in the face. Ethan took a step backward until he was standing directly next to the nightstand, and Grady knew he had one last confession to make.

"Open the drawer," he said, nodding toward the piece of furniture behind Ethan. Ethan hesitated but then did as he was told. Inside he found a pistol and he carefully took it out.

"That's how I was going to kill Marius," Grady informed him. At this point, he knew he'd already lost Ethan forever so he might as well put everything out on the table. He had nothing left to lose.

"Inside, you'll find it's loaded with a silver bullet," Grady continued. "It's no standard issue one, either. It has been both blessed by monks, which is a feat of its own accord, and has had powerful magic placed upon it. The result is that it's one of a kind and will not miss its target. Marius would be dead in an instant."

Ethan held the gun timidly.

"Where would you even get something like that?"

"Sozopol, Bulgaria. I had to give up a piece of my soul to obtain it. If I were a lesser man than I already am, I suppose I would blame that as the reason for my cruelty, but we're both too smart to believe that."

Ethan gulped. "You can barter *pieces* of your soul?"

"Everything is for sale when you deal with devils," Grady answered solemnly.

"I thought you didn't believe in God."

"I wasn't talking about God."

"So, that's it then," Ethan said angrily. "You were going to hijack me and have me take you to the Dream World so you could shoot Marius? That's what all of this has been about?"

"Yes."

"And what if it didn't kill him? What was the plan then?"

Again, Grady found himself longing for Ethan to have been far less perceptive.

"If I couldn't exact my revenge then I was prepared to die at the hands of the monster that killed the woman I loved. One of us would have to die. For us to both live felt like sickening injustice," Grady answered.

"And there it is," Ethan spat. "You were willing to sacrifice me for some pathetic Shakespearian death. How poetic of you, Grady! We both know if you had died there, I wouldn't have been able to save myself. You saw me with that vampire. I would have been dead if it weren't for you. But now, I guess I would've ended up dead *because* of you as well."

Grady thought he saw an aura of white light slowly starting to form around Ethan. He recognized his emotions were causing the energy around him to shift and change. For fear another psychic pulse was about to burst forward, Grady tried to diffuse his anger.

"That's why I told you, Ethan," he said. "I couldn't go through with any of it. Once you were a real person to me all of those plans inside of my head voided out, I knew I could never betray you."

"You already had!"

"I promise you, everything that occurred after we met wasn't part of the plan. You have fundamentally changed me!" Grady insisted.

"After a week?" Ethan scoffed. "People don't change that quickly."

"Don't they? Are you not a different man today than you were before we met?"

"Oh, I'm definitely a different man now," Ethan's tone was laced with warning.

"I love you, Ethan. With every piece of my heart and soul I still have left to give!" Grady pleaded. "I could never risk hurting you."

"Oh, really?" Ethan sneered. "Tell me then, Grady, why you still felt the need to hypnotize me last night? When did you decide you would shower me with your loving mercy? Was it before we talked about hope on the balcony, or after you kissed me for the first time? When *exactly* did I earn a pass from death from you?"

Grady couldn't bear the torture of the moment anymore. He swiftly moved towards Ethan to try to comfort him. He was immediately stopped in his tracks as Ethan pulled the gun on him and, while he didn't cock it, his thumb hovered decisively close to it.

"I performed the hypnotism for the exact reason I told you. I swear it!" Grady said, careful to remain as still as possible. "It was to give you an anchor. To help you control your situation."

"Dacey said this is what you do." His voice was thick with bitterness. "You break people's hearts."

"I never intended that," Grady insisted. "I didn't know how any of this would play out. I honestly don't think I ever could have risked your life, even if I hadn't fallen in love with you. I could never harm someone as innocent as you."

"Shut up, okay?" Ethan shouted. His hand was trembling and he lowered the gun. Grady knew Ethan was too kind of a person to ever use it but a wave of relief washed over him just the same. Ethan's body was shaking with emotion. "You want to die so badly, Grady? Do you really think that would create any sort of balance in the world?"

"At this point, I'm starting to believe the world might be better without me in it," Grady confessed softly.

"Stop!" Ethan exclaimed in frustration. The psychic pulse that had been building finally shot out of him and knocked Grady onto the ground. He stared up at Ethan with genuine fascination and partial fear.

"Why do you *always* say these awful things about yourself? It's like a sick self-fulfilling prophecy," Ethan cried.

"I thought you would feel the same way. That you would want me gone," Grady answered softly, glancing at the pistol in his hand.

"I don't want you dead, Grady." Ethan rolled his eyes. "I'm not as twisted as you are. You know, we all have bad shit that happens to us. That doesn't mean you go out and hurt other people, or yourself, or manifest intricate schemes to get yourself killed. It means you strive to overcome it! You try to be better than the thing that's knocked you down."

For once, Grady was truly speechless. He knew Ethan was completely right.

"I *believed* in you," Ethan said. "I believed you were better. Sure, I thought your treatment of supernaturals was misguided, but I believed in your intentions. Why? Because I thought they came from a good place. I thought you wanted to save the world! Now I see a man who wants to destroy it because it broke his heart once. So, you know what? *I'm* going to be the hero now. And you don't *get* to die! You don't get to have your carefully orchestrated tragedy. You don't get that satisfaction."

Then he did something purely amazing. Ethan managed to warp the world in front of him. Grady saw reality split open, like a curtain being drawn, and a dark void of nothingness stood in its place. Ethan threw the pistol into the black abyss. With a flick of his wrist reality sewed itself back together. The gun was gone forever. Where had it gone? That was a question they'd probably never find the answer to. It simply no longer existed.

"My God..." Grady was dumbfounded.

"You were right about one thing," Ethan said with newly found confidence. He glared down at Grady, "I *am* better than you. And more powerful than you. And I was willing to love you forever. I *loved* you. And now you have to live with that."

It was the final blow Grady couldn't handle. He was consumed with sorrow for the consequences of his actions. So this was to be his punishment? To lose the chance at love again? Most people were lucky to find it once. He'd had the rare gift of a second chance but had doomed it from the start with his self-centered immorality.

WHAT HE DIDN'T see was that Ethan paused. For a split second, he wanted nothing more than to go back to how things were. He wanted to lift Grady up and rebuild him in a better form than what he'd been, but the fury of treachery still waged war within him and he knew he had to leave before something even more terrible transpired.

So, Ethan left. His body pulled in a dozen different directions from the inside as his emotions caused his powers to manifest in ways they never had before. As he shut Grady's door behind him, he was swooped up off of his feet. He stood shakily in the air as he attempted to recalibrate his balance. He was levitating. Thankfully, no one else was around to witness it. He secretly thanked Grady for marking the second floor "off limits" during the party. Now the only problem was trying to figure out how to get his feet back on the ground.

He took a careful step forward and found himself walking on air. There was no way he could go downstairs or even risk leaving the house if he was going to be floating. That would definitely draw attention. Instead, he delicately made his way to his own room and locked himself inside.

Ethan desperately wished he could leave the house and all of its memories behind him. At least for tonight. The truth about Grady and his own foolhardy misplaced trust in him made him ashamed. He had been an idiot. No, he'd been naïve, like everyone always said he was.

The annoyance of this thought caused yet another psychic pulse, but this one was milder and only ended up sending himself toppling over backward in mid-air. He nearly overturned his dresser as his hip bumped into it.

He knew he had to get his powers under control and fast. However, it was too much to ask to try to control his emotions when he was still trying to work through them. He hated Grady for putting him through this. The anger sent him toppling over again.

Then he realized something he hadn't expected at all. He didn't hate Grady. He, surprisingly, pitied him. He was furious he'd been manipulated but deep down he believed Grady was remorseful. Why else would he have come clean and not gone through with his plan?

This momentary understanding and acceptance brought Ethan some peace of mind and he was able to feel his feet touch the floor once again.

"Great." He rolled his eyes. "So if I want to have control then I have to rob myself of the right to be upset? Isn't that just the way."

A knock came at his door and his heart rate increased rapidly, nearly sending him floating up again.

"Go away!" Ethan commanded. "I locked the door for a reason, Grady! Leave me alone!"

"It's not Grady," a female voice responded kindly. It was Vivian.

Ethan was tempted to yell at her to go away anyway but he didn't want to be rude. He also didn't want to make the effort to cross the room so he absentmindedly pretended to open the lock on the door and was surprised when he saw his intention caused it to open for itself.

"Come in!" He grasped his hands together in an attempt to control them and hoped he didn't do anything weird while she was there.

Vivian peeked through the door as she cracked it open and then slowly entered, shutting it behind her.

"What are you doing up here?" Ethan asked nervously.

"I was in the foyer and heard a crashing noise. I thought I should come and check on you."

Ethan fumbled for an answer. "Oh, I...I tripped into my, uhm, dresser."

"Actually, I think it was Grady." She motioned in the direction of the other man's room. "It sounds like he's throwing things in there."

"Oh..." Ethan responded dismally.

She cocked her head. "Are you okay?"

"Yeah." Ethan tried to assure her but he couldn't plaster on the fake smile he was trying to conjure up, "No...I don't know."

She considered him with a sympathetic gaze and then gave him a huge hug.

"I know we haven't had a chance to get too close but, believe me, I know what you're going through."

"I really don't think you do," he retorted.

She considered him knowingly. "I've been through this before. When Grady and Marguerite were together. Trust me, there were many ice cream filled conversations after they fought."

"I don't like ice cream," Ethan said flatly.

"Who doesn't like ice cream?"

He began listing off in an effort to divert the topic. "People with milk allergies, the lactose intolerant, vegans…"

Vivian laughed.

"You're cute. Seriously, though, Marguerite was my best friend. So, I know how tough Grady can be to navigate sometimes. Especially in matters of the heart."

"Did he love her?" Ethan asked spitefully. A huge part of him wanted Grady to have never loved anyone. Including him.

"No, not at all. That was their problem."

"So he was using her."

"No. He wasn't anything-ing her."

Ethan was confused.

Vivian pursed her lips. "She meant nothing to him but he meant the world to her. That's why it didn't work out and that's why they don't get along now."

"I thought they didn't get along because she tried to curse him and inadvertently ended up cursing Benny."

"Well, that's part of it too. There's a lot of he-said she-said to the story," Vivian admitted. "Would you like to get out of here? Maybe some fresh air will help clear your head?"

"You don't mind? What about Thomas?"

"He's fine. Caught up in a conversation with Arthur. Apparently, they're both rather unfond of Grady at the moment."

"We should form a club," Ethan joked. It was a joke that killed him inside to say. The pain of anger at the man he loved stung so deeply he wanted to collapse to the floor in tears. But with Vivian standing before him, he was able to keep his emotions in check.

Vivian and Ethan covertly made their way downstairs and managed to make a quiet exit from the house without notice. The cool air of the night kissed Ethan's cheeks and the chill reminded him of tears that had been there minutes before.

He hesitated before getting into Vivian's car as he stared at the full moon that hung brilliantly contrasted against the dark sky. How surreal it was to think he had almost met his death tonight because of it. If Grady had of been a worse man than he already was.

Yes, he would be glad to get away for a while.

Ethan got in the car and smiled thankfully at Vivian.

"I really appreciate you being so nice to me," he said.

"Aww," she cooed. "You're so sweet. It almost makes me feel bad I have to do this."

Before he had time to react, she conjured a glowing purple orb that blasted into him. It threw his body forward and his head smashed into the dashboard, leaving him limp.

Everything went black.

Seventeen: The Taste of Death

WHEN ETHAN OPENED his eyes, he wasn't anywhere he recognized. In fact, he wasn't anywhere at all. Well, he was somewhere and it was like being everywhere all at once. He was floating in a vast abyss surrounded by star clusters. They were made of brilliant purples, blues, and reds and hung in the open space around him like anchored clouds. He was lost in the universe.

Fear gripped him as he wondered if he might be lost forever and the terror propelled him forward. He was swimming through the vastness of space and he had never been so free. His fear subsided and was replaced with awe and excitement. These emotions allowed something incredible to happen.

Consciousnesses, hundreds of them, became present before him. They began to multiply until there were millions. They were like puffs of ethereal smoke whirling all around him and when he focused on only one at a time then he discovered he could see into them clearly; like peeping through a keyhole. A familiar but far away city, a foreign world, someone else's dream, and perhaps someone's memory. He was seeing all of time and space at once. He reached out to one of the wisps as it flew by him and it halted course. Ethan hesitated, unsure of how dangerous it would be to actually touch one.

Before he could decide his next move, an excruciating pain engulfed him and he reached for his forehead instead.

The wisp floated away. The universe was breaking up. It was beginning to flash in and out of his sight like static on an old television. He had the familiar sensation of plummeting like the last time he returned from the Dream World. In moments, he was back in his body and staring into a dark room that was lit only by a circle of purple and black candles, surrounding him.

When he removed his hand from his forehead, he saw blood on his fingers and remembered Vivian attacking him in the car. He surveyed his surroundings and listened intently. No one else was there at the moment and from what he could tell of the flickering light given off by the burning wicks, he was imprisoned in a basement somewhere. There was a staircase, no windows, and his ankles had been shackled to the floor with short chains.

His foot had healed up from his previous injury but the grasp of the metal around his skin made phantom pains revive their anguish. Thankfully, his hands were free. Vivian obviously didn't realize how Ethan's powers worked. Then again, Ethan wasn't even sure if Vivian knew he had powers. Why in the world had she kidnapped him? And where had she taken him?

Careful to be as quiet as possible, as he assumed he'd been left alone since he had been unconscious, Ethan pulled his phone from his pocket. Another blessing! She hadn't thought to take it from him. *Amateur*, Ethan thought snidely. He usually wouldn't be so self-assured in this kind of situation, but learning he was a supernatural being who could travel over dimensional boundaries had given him somewhat of an instantaneous and well-deserved ego. His sudden blossoming of self-confidence caused him to recall Grady's earlier remarks about how a person could change so vastly in such a short amount of time.

Grady. Ethan's heart sunk. If only he could have controlled his emotions when the other man was confessing his transgressions. Perhaps things would've ended differently. Perhaps they still could.

Ethan covertly swiped his phone on and opened his Maps application, saying a silent prayer the location would work. It did. He zoomed in on the address of the pinpoint to discover he was indeed somewhere he'd been before. Marguerite's shop. *They were working together*, he reasoned.

He listened again to hear if anyone was moving around upstairs but it was still deadly silent. This was it. He had to take the risk. He thought about dialing 911 but explaining he was trapped in a witch's shop might sound like a hoax; not to mention, how would they stop them when they arrived? They weren't exactly equipped to deal with magic. No, he had to call someone who could handle the situation. He dialed Grady.

The call went directly to voice mail. *Dammit! Quit wallowing and turn on your fucking phone!* Ethan thought angrily. He wasn't going to waste his one chance to be vocal on a message that might be heard far too late. He'd have to think of something else.

A drop of blood rolled off his forehead and onto his sweater sleeve and suddenly he knew exactly who to reach out to. *Thank goodness for horny vampires*, Ethan thought as he pressed the contact Dacey had entered on his phone the first time they met.

MARCUS HAD ALREADY taken off and Dacey had diverted his attention to attempting to seduce Karen Roam. He was in the middle of complementing the curves of her bosom in her medieval dress, much to her amusement and Arthur's umbrage, when his phone began buzzing in his pocket. He pulled it out, expecting it to be Marcus begging him to reconsider joining him in Dallas, but instead saw it wasn't a number he recognized. He did have a bad habit of giving his number out to anyone he found even remotely attractive, though, so he excused himself from the group and answered the call with eager curiosity.

"Hello?"

"Dacey! It's Ethan," a hushed voice came through.

"Ethan! When I said to call me some time, I didn't expect it to be at your own party while you're toying away with your boyfriend. Or...is this a request for a rendezvous of the *ménage* à *trois* variety? If so, then my answer is yes."

"Dacey, shut up and listen to me, please!"

Dacey frowned. "You sound displeased."

"I am. I am *very* displeased at the moment. Now listen—I need you to get Grady and come down to Marguerite's shop as fast as you two can! Short story: Vivian kidnapped me and now I'm trapped in the basement. I'm not really sure what they're planning but kidnappings don't usually involve happy endings."

"I've known some that have."

"Dacey!" Ethan reprimanded.

"You're serious? You've really been kidnapped by that basic witch?"

"Yes!" Ethan said, "Look, I have to go before they realize I'm awake. They have me in chains and surrounded with candles. I don't know if that helps in figuring out what they might be up to but please, find Grady and get over here."

The call disconnected.

"Candles and chains," Dacey repeated to himself. "His night is sounding so much more interesting than mine."

All joking aside, the vampire did realize the severity of the situation and quickly made his way upstairs. Grady's door was closed so he rapped his knuckles on it to see if the man would respond.

He did. Rather quickly. Obviously, in hopes it was someone else because when he saw Dacey standing there instead he slammed the door shut.

"Oh, come on!" Dacey rolled his eyes and opened the door to let himself in.

"Go away, Dacey," Grady sighed as he sat on the edge of his bed, staring intently at the floor. Dacey assessed the room. It was a wreck. Indiscernible objects had been broken and their pieces were scattered all around. Grady's nightstand had even been toppled over.

"I see you still like it rough," Dacey said with a smirk.

"I said go away," Grady repeated defensively.

"What's that pitiful expression I spy?" Dacey asked, kneeling down in front of the other man to search his face, "Is it guilt? Guilt is one of my favorite human emotions. It drives men mad."

"Clearly," Grady retorted. Surprisingly, for the first time since they'd known each other, Grady let his boundaries down and opened his eyes to Dacey, allowing the telepathic vampire to read him without attempting to block anything out. It was the first gesture of trust Dacey had ever received from the man. It also caused him to become crestfallen as he read everything that had transpired.

"Love, I'm so sorry," he said, taking Grady's hand.

But Grady pulled away. "What did I expect? Acceptance? Forgiveness? Of course he was going to leave."

"Well, I don't know if he left so much as—" Dacey started to say as he stood upright to explain the situation but Grady interrupted him.

"No, he did. He left," Grady sighed again with tears in his eyes. "I went to offer another apology and he was gone. I don't know why I thought he'd still be here...I would give anything for him to still be here."

"I must say, you're very off-putting when you're depressed," Dacey remarked. He wasn't overly fond of engaging in human dramatics. Grady glared at him.

"You're not entirely innocent in all this," Grady countered with a miffed tone. "He said you told him breaking hearts is *"what I do"*."

"I also said you didn't do it intentionally." Dacey was quick to defend himself. How could Ethan use his own words against him? Very rude, to say the least. "Why is he dragging *me* into your domestic disputes? The only way I get drawn into other people's relationships is in the bedroom."

"Technically, the dispute *did* happen in a bedroom," Grady pointed out.

"Yes, well, you can only blame me so far. This mess was entirely your design."

Grady didn't have a response for that.

"But now is your chance to make things better! Seize the day! Or night, as it were! *Carpe Noctem*! Be the hero and save your lover in distress."

"What are you talking about? I'm the one that distressed him," Grady argued. "The last person he wants around is me."

"That's not what he said," Dacey finally revealed. "He specifically requested I tell you to come save him. I think he insinuated I should come along as well, so I think I may. I heard there were chains involved which sounds highly titillating."

Grady stood up abruptly with concern. "You talked to him? When? What chains?"

"Oh, he just called me," Dacey answered nonchalantly. "Something about Vivian had kidnapped him and he was stuck in Marguerite's basement. He wanted us to come save him and I think he mentioned a *ménage* à *trois* would occur at some point as well."

Grady frantically reached into his pocket and turned on his phone, no doubt to see if he'd missed a call from Ethan. "Why didn't you tell me this first?" Grady asked angrily, as he grabbed one of his lined jackets from his closet and began running around the room stocking it up with various effects that could only be weaponry and defenses.

"You're right. The threesome should have been the lead-in."

Grady rounded on him.

Dacey sighed. *Why does he need weapons when he's already glaring daggers?* "Darling heart, I did try but you were too inconsolable to listen to what I was intending to say." Dacey picked up a vial filled with a thick amber liquid of some sort and turned it upside down to watch it slowly roll to the opposite end. Grady snatched it out of his hand and stuffed it into the jacket, finally throwing the garment on and making his way out of the room.

"How does one listen to what someone *intends* to say? What does that even mean?" Grady shook his head with annoyance as Dacey followed eagerly behind him.

Dacey shrugged. "I guess it's a telepathic thing."

Grady abruptly halted and spun on his heel to face him.

"You're not going," he ordered.

"What? Of course I am! He said *we* should come and save him."

"Whatever Marguerite is up to isn't going to end well," Grady stated with all seriousness. "I don't know if she's manipulated Vivian in some way or if they were always working together. Whatever the case, she's obviously been planning this for a while. The stars aligned for her as they had for me. There is a very real possibility...No. It's an almost certain *fact* not everyone will survive this encounter. I won't have any more lives at risk on my watch. You're not going."

"Please," Dacey said, brushing off Grady's stalwart concern. "We both know you can use all the help you can get. You'll be up against two witches who already know all of your tricks. Besides, what life is at risk? I'm already dead."

Grady seemed to search Dacey's eyes for a way to discourage him from joining the fight so Dacey solidified his intentions with his next statement.

"I care about Ethan too," Dacey stated sincerely.

Grady offered a grim but firm nod of acceptance and the two made their way down the stairs and to the front door, completely ignoring the party that waged on in the rest of the house.

"Where do you think you two are going?" Arthur's voice called out as he approached them heading out. He scanned the large foyer, then glanced up the stairs, and then to Grady with suspicion, "Where's Ethan?"

"I don't have time for this, Arthur," Grady responded in frustration.

Arthur grabbed Grady firmly by the arm and gruffly demanded, "*Where* is Ethan?"

"Sorry, old sport, I'm afraid he's been kidnapped by a couple of wicked witches and we're on our way to save him. We'll give him your regards, though." Dacey grinned cordially. Arthur was obviously shocked and Grady glared at Dacey with indignation.

"What? He wasn't going to leave us alone about it and we need to hurry. Just speeding the process along," Dacey explained as a matter-of-fact.

"I'm going with you," Arthur said, moving to follow them. Grady forcibly stopped him in his tracks.

"Have you gone mad?" he asked. "You wouldn't stand a chance in a fight with most regular men. What makes you think you can take on the supernatural? Dacey and I will handle this. You're more of a help here. Watch over Karen and make sure she doesn't suspect anything is wrong. As far as everyone in that house is concerned, Ethan and I have stolen away upstairs for the night and won't be back down."

"I've stolen away with them," Dacey added. "You can add that part into the story as well."

Grady ignored him and continued his instructions, "Play host and excuse them all when the time is right. Please, don't let anyone know something is awry. Those beasts in there must think I'm still present to punish them if they get out of control."

"Did you tell him?" Arthur asked.

"Yes," Grady confirmed. "That's part of the reason we're in this mess. Now, please, I implore you to stay here and hold up this facade before any more of it starts crumbling down around me."

Arthur apparently chose to believe in Grady, at least one last time, and nodded in dutiful agreement. When he turned to reenter the house, the three of them saw Thomas standing in the doorway. He'd overheard everything.

"Witches?" he asked, his face lined with worry. "Like Vivian?"

"Vivian exactly, in fact," Dacey said.

Grady watched the man intently and Dacey could hear his mind whirring with suspicion he might be in on it too. Though the expression on Thomas's face read negative.

"That can't be," Thomas said. "Vivian wouldn't do that."

"Is she here?" Grady shouted with irritation, throwing his hands up to accentuate the obvious betrayal. "She fooled us all. I'm sorry Thomas. I'm sorry for anything I might have to do tonight."

Grady turned and set off for his Jaguar but Thomas came bounding up behind him and ran around to the passenger side, opening up the door to get in.

"I'm going," Thomas stated firmly.

"No fair! I didn't know there'd be three of us or I would've called shotgun!" Dacey protested as he got in the backseat.

"What's with everyone demanding to throw themselves into the face of certain death tonight?" Grady complained as he got behind the steering wheel.

"Well, it is Samhain, after all," Dacey pointed out as they sped off into the night to rescue their friend. "'Tis the reason for the season."

AS SOON AS Ethan hung up on Dacey, he began working on how to free himself from the chains that bound him to the cold floor. He ran his hands over the metal cuffs that gripped his ankles. He knew he should be able to unlock them with his powers but he hadn't yet learned how to control them. Everything he'd done so far had happened as second nature. It had all been instantaneous instinct. Now he was actively trying to force it to work, nothing seemed to be happening.

He heard movement from upstairs and his heart began to race. He didn't have much time to free himself. *Let go, let go, let go*, he begged the cuffs inwardly but they remained in place. He recalled unlocking his bedroom door with the flick of his wrist. In that moment, he had used a fluid motion; one that seemed effortless.

Ethan ignored the sounds emanating from above and focused solely on the one goal of freeing himself. With a smooth gesture he motioned with his hands for the cuffs to come free and, surprisingly, they fell off, rattling on the floor beside him. His momentary excitement was quickly stifled as the door of the basement opened.

Thinking fast, he scooped the chains up underneath himself and sat cross-legged so it would seem he were still restrained. He carefully watched two forms in black cloaks descending the stairs. One held a bowl and the other held a ceremonial knife.

The hooded figures silently approached him and then the knife-wielding one pulled back her hood to reveal herself. It was Marguerite. The other figure stayed hooded but Ethan could see in the flickering light of the candlelit room it was Vivian.

"I'm so glad to see you've joined us again," Marguerite said with a cruel smile as she stood before him. "That makes things a little easier. We are on a tight schedule, after all."

Vivian knelt down on the floor beside them, placing the bowl of water in front of her. At least, Ethan assumed it was water. It was some form of clear liquid, anyway. He stared at her with pleading eyes.

"Vivian, what's going on?" he asked. He didn't expect a pleasant response but he at least wanted to know why she'd attacked him and brought him here. Vivian wasn't the one to answer him, though.

"I'm afraid your friend is working on autopilot now," Marguerite said. "She was always pretty easy to manipulate."

Ethan glared at her. "You've put a spell on her?"

"Hello. Witch!" Marguerite retorted affirmatively. She then reached out with the knife and softly ran it along his forehead. She didn't cut him with it but instead used the edge to gather some of the blood he'd already lost.

A chill ran up his spine as she caressed him with the blade. He thought about jumping forward to attack her but then decided he was in too close of stabbing range to take the chance.

She dabbed the tip of the blade into the bowl and Ethan saw his own blood begin to swirl around as if an invisible being were stirring it.

"What do you want with me?" he asked her coldly.

"What do *I* want with you?" she repeated, as if she were actually pondering the statement for the first time. "*I* want to see you scream. *I* want to see you in pain. *I* want to stick this knife through your precious little heart and then leave it on Grady's front doorstep!"

She accentuated the last sentence by pressing the tip of the knife into Ethan's chest, causing him to cringe with fear. Her eyes were wild and full of murderous passion.

"But...this isn't about what I want," she continued. "There's a bigger plan you and I are both lucky to be a part of. You see, we don't need Grady anymore. He's nothing to us now."

"What are you talking about?" he asked, partially to hear whatever insanity she was willing to offer up and partially to buy time until he figured out an escape plan. His idea of employing the element of surprise by lunging at her, free from the chains, was dashed as she unexpectedly hopped into his lap.

Marguerite straddled Ethan in a sickly seductive way that made an already terrifying situation even more disturbing to him. She kept the tip of the blade pressed against his chest which prevented him from trying to maneuver away from her. She stared into his eyes with what seemed like hateful curiosity. "Why would he want you?" she seemed to ask herself. "He had me. Why would he want a little boy like you?"

Ethan's heart was racing. Marguerite was legitimately insane, and with every word she seemed to not only press the tip of the knife against him more harshly but also press herself against him more firmly as well. He was pretty sure if he didn't play along she would probably go through with her fantasy of impaling his heart on her blade.

"I...I don't know," he responded shakily.

"Does he love you?" A rage filled her eyes as she dared him to put the nail in his own coffin and answer 'yes'.

"I don't think so," he lied. The spark in her eyes faded a bit and, with it, so did the pressure of the blade's tip. She relaxed and pulled the knife away. Ethan breathed a heavy sigh of relief.

"You poor thing," she said, her voice transitioning from passionate anger to pity. "I've been there. He'll use you all up, you know? He'll take all of your love and never give any in return. Did he do that to you too? He did that to me. He tried to *reform* me; to make me normal. I couldn't turn my back on who I was, though, and he shunned me for that. He threw me out like I was trash. All for being myself. But not before taking my body, my passion, my love... He got everything he could have wanted from me and I wound up with nothing. I bet that's what he did to you."

Ethan gulped down his disgust. The only thing sparing his life at this moment was some twisted assumption Marguerite had made that they were somehow on the same side in hating Grady.

Hadn't it been true, though? Is that not how I'd felt earlier tonight? Of course, it wasn't the same as anything Marguerite had experienced, he reminded himself. That's what made him so sick. The truth was, Grady *did* love him and despite all of his mistakes, all of his faults, and all of his lies...Ethan knew he still loved Grady too. But now his life depended on him stringing along Grady's ex-lover. *How many of those does he have exactly?* Hopefully, he wouldn't encounter any more of them and, if he did, then hopefully it wouldn't end up like this. That is, if he even survived the night to meet them someday.

"We...don't need him," Ethan reminded her as he played along. That's what she'd said. He wanted her to explain that part.

She beamed. "That's right!" If he were even remotely attracted to psycho women on the verge of killing him then he might have thought her strikingly gorgeous in that moment. That's when he realized she assumed he did find her attractive. She kept heaving her breasts closer to him as she spoke and grinding into his lap as if *that* would somehow sway him to take her side, not the fact she was imminently stab-happy. He wondered if she had succeeded in having a relationship with Grady in the past because he fell victim to her feminine wiles or her psychotic episodes. He honestly couldn't put anything past Grady anymore. "I met someone new," she continued. "I've been amping up my psychic abilities and I contacted someone from the other side. And wouldn't you know, it's a small world there too! He knew all about you! No one could have guessed the key would come waltzing into my shop but I read it in the cards before you left. It was destiny. Grady had taken everything from me and now karma has delivered me this chance to take everything from him."

Ethan was perplexed which seemed to please her. He could tell because she wrapped her arms around his shoulders as though she were about to kiss him.

"Isn't it funny how things play out sometimes?" she said in a sing-song voice. "You and I ended up in the same place. Right when he needed us. Right where we're supposed to be."

"In a basement?" Ethan asked sarcastically. He was growing tired of her games and wishing for an opportunity to escape her physical advances.

Her eyes flickered wildly again. "Are you mocking me?"

"Who did you meet?" Ethan asked in an effort to distract her from her resumed anger.

"Oh, you'll find out soon enough," she answered with a wicked smile. "You're going to help him return home and then we'll all rule this world and its pathetic people together. He will be a god amongst men and you and I will be royalty."

"I'm already a god amongst men," Ethan countered bravely. This arrogant statement apparently thrilled Marguerite and Ethan immediately regretted saying it as it only seemed to turn her on more.

"Are you now?" she whispered into his ear seductively. She dropped the blade to the floor and reached down to his pants, unbuckling the slim belt he had on.

"Show me," she breathed again. "Show me what Grady saw in you."

Her unwanted touch incited the exact emotions he needed to take advantage of the situation and a pulse of energy built up inside him.

"Sure thing...you crazy bitch!" he shouted as the psychic blast released itself from the aura of his body and threw her across the room. Ethan scrambled to his feet and grabbed the knife while he had a chance. He turned to run and was immediately knocked back by another blast. This time it came in the form of a purple ball of energy from an enraged Marguerite. His back hit the wall and he crumpled to the floor, losing his grip on the knife. She advanced on him too quickly for him to get another attack in.

"I think it's time to bring our new friend home." Her voice was cruel as she placed her hand in the center of his forehead and knocked him to sleep with a spell.

This time when Ethan opened his eyes, he wasn't floating around in the universe. He was in the Dream World. He reasoned this meant sleep was the access point to dreams, whereas a forced unconsciousness accessed something else entirely. It also didn't take him very long to figure out the "friend" of Marguerite's had to be Marius. She was the one who had connected with him and given him the extra push he needed to attempt an escape.

He was now amongst the wooded landscape and quickly moved to duck behind a tree so that he wouldn't be so easily noticeable. *Is Marius already expecting me?* The odds definitely leaned in favor of it as everyone had kept making such a big deal to him about how this night was the opportune moment to use him as a vehicle. He was sure Marius had helped Marguerite orchestrate his capture.

Ethan knew someone was watching him. He had that inexplicable sensation of being observed.

"You came back," a familiar female voice said. That's when the fox trotted up next to him. Ethan was relieved but still on guard. He noticed something about the animal he hadn't the first time; then again, it had been on a ledge above him last. Now he could see a full view of it and it was glaringly obvious this fox had three tails.

"Not by choice," he answered honestly.

"It's happened. He's using you," she said.

"He's trying to," Ethan confirmed. "But I'm not going to let him."

"Have you finally learned the truth?" she asked hopefully.

"Yes. All of it. What I am. Everything I can do. What they want with me."

He thought he saw the fox smile.

Then, her body began to morph and grow. The transition wasn't as forced or grotesque as when Benny had changed. It was quite the opposite; effortless and with an ethereal grace. The red haired girl with the kind blue eyes and subtle freckles stood before him.

"I know what I am," Ethan said. "Please, tell me who...or what you are."

"I'm Avandalmischa, a kitsune. Your father called me Kit and so you may as well. I'm a creature of this world and I was Vincent's ally."

Marius had yet to show any signs of being around, so Ethan relaxed from his rigid position against the tree. There was so much he wanted to ask Kit and now he finally had the chance.

"You're from this place? Are there more of you? I've only ever seen you."

"There are plenty of us," Kit responded. "We can only be seen by those that we wish to see us and in whatever form we choose."

"Well, that explains how you knew my father but still look like you're as young as I am." He'd already learned with vampires that you could never judge someone's age by their appearance.

"You said you were allies. In what?"

"Your father's goal was to rid your world of the monsters who would seek to rain terror upon it. He would capture them and bring them to my world where I would keep guard until he was able to determine their dimension of origin. He would then return and take them to their rightful places."

"So, he didn't kill them. He relocated things. He traveled," Ethan realized. His father's goal was so similar to Grady's but the follow through was extremely different. He imagined implementing this kind of plan with Grady at his side. They could change the world together, like Vincent and Kit had attempted to do.

She nodded. "He roamed all realities with the single purpose of bringing balance."

"Roam," Ethan said with a smirk. Of course. His name was as made-up as Grady's. He should have guessed.

"Marius was his last drop off. He never returned to take him," Kit finished. Her eyes were filled with sadness.

"He died soon after I was born," Ethan confirmed.

"I assumed as much. What he was doing was dangerous. Obviously, there were many who disagreed with him. I also knew he was to have a child. He had mentioned it. So, I waited. I hoped you'd find yourself here someday. Now you can finish what he started."

Ethan wasn't safe from anyone. Everyone was asking him to do the same thing tonight. Take them places. He could see this easily being the most annoying thing about his powers. Interdimensional superhuman taxi service.

"You want me to take Marius back to whatever dimension werewolves originally came from?" Ethan asked her with exasperation. "I can't. I have no idea how to do that or where that even is. I'm not my father."

She seemed disappointed but then a new determination washed over her.

"Then be different than him. Kill Marius."

"*You* kill Marius," he countered. "Why is he my problem?"

"Kitsune cannot kill. If we do, we cease to exist."

"Oh..." Ethan didn't have an appropriate response but it didn't really matter if he did because he wouldn't have had time to say it anyway.

Branches cracked and fell as the large black wolf bounded at them through the foliage. His snarling intensified as he reached forward to lash out at them. Kit and Ethan took off at a sprint, propelling themselves forward as fast as they could go in order to escape the surprise attack.

"Guess he didn't like all that 'kill him' talk!" Ethan shouted to Kit as they ran through the seemingly endless forest. They maneuvered through the brush and trees as quickly as possible but the wolf was gaining ground.

With imminent death on his heels and everything he'd learned tonight, Ethan was able to see the situation clearly. Whether or not he'd met Grady, he still would've ended up here; in this place, with this problem. It was inevitable. He regretted running away from Grady and destroying the one magical weapon that might have actually saved his life. At least with them he would've stood a chance. Now, he was faced with the same monster but without weapons and with a weird fox lady at his side. There was no way he could see himself making it out of this alive. For all he knew, his destiny had included Grady as his one option for survival and he'd thrown it away.

Kit leaped up in the air and grabbed onto a branch, limberly pulling herself up into a tree. Ethan was both surprised by her quick escape and jealous he didn't possess the same cirque-like skills. He wondered if he would be able to make himself levitate in the Dream World. Maybe he could float away like a balloon. He was about to try it as the wolf pounced on him from behind, toppling him to the ground.

"Come home, Ethan!" a disembodied voice shouted. It echoed through his mind and hoped surged within him as it drew him back.

"Grady!" Ethan nearly cried with relief. They had made it. They had found him.

Ethan's body ripped away from the Dream World and began to plummet to reality when he saw the horror of what was happening. Marius had gotten exactly what he wanted. A free ride. The wolf had attached himself to Ethan and was falling into their world with him.

"No!" Ethan screamed. His eyes flew open to see Grady huddled down before him as he'd been trying to wake him up. Dacey was near the staircase fighting with Marguerite. She was launching spell after spell at him but he moved too fast for her and knocked her to the ground as he bared his fangs. Vivian was collapsed on the floor; Ethan couldn't tell if she were alive or dead, but Thomas was trying desperately to revive her.

In a matter of seconds, as if manifesting from nothing, Marius appeared directly by Ethan. He stood at full form, looming down menacingly above them all and howled victoriously. Everyone froze as they took in the terrifying sight of their new foe. Except for Marguerite who grinned insanely and used the distraction to push Dacey off of her. She scrambled to her feet and ran toward the wolf.

"I knew it!" she cried out excitedly. "I did it!"

The towering wolf turned his attention to her keenly as he finally saw the face of his accomplice. His eyes were full of darkness and a cold evil Ethan had never seen before. Grady grabbed Ethan's arm and whisked him away from the monster in an effort to protect him.

"Yes, you served your purpose," the wolf growled at Marguerite.

She reached out to him as a sign of camaraderie.

The wolf lunged forward at her and viciously tore off her head. The others cringed at the grisly sight and Marius spun to face Grady and Ethan.

"Give him to me or I'll kill you all!" he commanded, blood still dripping from his teeth.

Grady positioned himself in front of Ethan and fearlessly met the harrowing glare of the creature.

"Your threats won't work here, Marius!" Grady reached into his coat. "You've met the one room of people who aren't afraid to die."

Marius cocked his head at Grady as soon as the man spoke. He seemed to be puzzling out a memory in his mind until his eyes widened with a sick glee.

"I remember you," Marius growled, clearly reveling in the memory of the murder.

"Good. We have unfinished business," Grady said with a vicious but controlled resolve. He quickly pulled out a hand-sized triggered crossbow armed with an arrow, which had a small bulb tip filled with liquid silver, and shot it at Marius's right eye. The wolf howled out in agony and he quickly reloaded and shot him in the left eye as well.

The pain for the wolf must have been excruciating but it only worked to stoke his rage. Even without vision he could apparently still smell them and sense their whereabouts. He bounded forward in a murderous rage at Grady and Ethan, knocking them both to the floor and sending Ethan rolling off too far away to do anything but watch in horror as the wolf went in for the kill at Grady's neck.

Eighteen: Sweet Dreams are Made of This

WITH MARGUERITE OUT of the way, Dacey was free to react more quickly than Ethan could. He assaulted the massive wolf with a powerful lunge and bit deep into his shoulder. Marius was caught by surprise and reeled back trying to knock the vampire off of him.

Grady was able to struggle free from beneath the wolf's heavy body; Ethan ran over to help pull him to his feet.

"Wh-what's going on?" Vivian stammered as she finally gained consciousness. It seemed Marguerite's spell on her had broken when the witch died. Thomas scooped her up in his arms as if he already knew what Grady was about to say.

"Get her out of here!" Grady shouted. Thomas didn't have to be told twice. He lifted his girlfriend over his shoulder and carried her up the stairs and out to safety as fast as he could.

Dacey and Marius were still struggling with one another. The wolf's angry growls almost drowned the vampire out as he shouted between bites, "Don't just stand there, do something!"

Grady seemed at a loss. "There's nothing I can use that won't harm Dacey in the process. All I can do is weaken him. I don't have anything powerful enough to kill him!" Grady lamented. He frowned at Ethan with frustration. "Well, I did but…"

"Really?" Ethan countered incredulously, "You're going to bring that up right now?"

Dacey reached around and punched the werewolf in its snarling snout as it tried to gnaw at him.

"Yes, you do!" Dacey yelled. He seemed to be trying his best not to fall from his vantage point as Marius thrust his body in all directions in an attempt to knock him off. "Ethan is the weapon!"

"He's right!" Grady grabbed Ethan by the shoulders and stared deep into his eyes. "You can do it! Open a portal like you did at home!"

Ethan shook his head. "I can't do it on command."

"Yes, you can!" Grady implored. "Like you did with the pistol."

"But...what about Dacey?" He saw the sadness and acceptance that became prominent in Grady's gaze.

"Dacey already made his choice," Grady answered. "The weight of the world is on your shoulders. You *must* do this."

Ethan knew he was right and he didn't have much time. Any second the massive werewolf could break free of Dacey's reign over him. Grady gave him a final nod of encouragement.

Ethan faced Marius and breathed a deep and even breath, focusing all of his emotions into one spot. He raised his hands and boldly ripped reality in half. The veil tore away revealing the black abyss behind it.

"Now!" Grady shouted to the vampire.

Dacey bit into the werewolf's neck and pressured him forward. The wolf, unable to see where he was going, stumbled straight into the darkness behind the veil. Dacey dismounted before Marius fell in, and for a moment Ethan was overjoyed with relief. The moment was short-lived, though, as Marius reached out to steady himself and grabbed onto Dacey, taking the handsome raven haired vampire with him. In seconds, they were both gone.

"NO!" Ethan cried out. He ran forward toward the abyss in an effort to save his friend. Grady had to grab him in a firm hold.

"Close it!" Grady instructed.

"NO!" Ethan tried to fight Grady off of him but he knew the effort was worthless. Dacey was gone and he had no idea how to bring him home.

"Close it!" Grady yelled again. That's when Ethan saw the rip was expanding at a rapid rate. Soon, they would fall into it as well. Fear and anguish consuming him, Ethan harnessed his emotions and successfully sealed the veil of reality back together.

They were safe.

Grady let Ethan go and he fell to his knees. Hot tears burned the surface of his eyes and he leaned forward, pressing his fists into the ground. How could he have sealed such a tragic fate for someone who had only seen the best in him? Someone who was willing to die for him. And he had let him.

A new feeling washed over him. One that he'd seen Grady wear many times but up until this point, he had been unfamiliar with himself. Self-hatred.

The universe had made him a magnificent creature but at the same time it had cursed him. How many friends would he have to see die in order to protect him simply so he could exist? How was that fair? How was that balance? Was that why his father had really died? Because no one was left to protect him or because he couldn't live with the guilt anymore?

Loathing and sadness consumed him like a tidal wave breaking free of the sea. His emotions caused the foundation of concrete beneath him to crack. His lifeboat finally came in the warm embrace of the only man who could possibly know what he was feeling.

"Let's get you out of here," Grady said softly, pulling Ethan up from the ground.

ETHAN SAT ON the steps in front of the witch's shop, staring up at the full moon that hung above him. The Killing Moon. He'd managed to survive it but not without great cost.

He'd checked the time on his phone. It was after midnight. Halloween was over and all of its horrors remained behind him but would never be forgotten.

He wondered where Thomas had taken Vivian. He'd probably run away to someplace he thought would be safe.

Grady had asked him to wait outside as he dealt with the gory duty of dealing with Marguerite's body and cleaning up the wreckage of the attack. Ethan wasn't really sure what that entailed and he honestly didn't even want to know. That was one secret he was fine with Grady keeping.

His eyelids were puffy and pink from crying, although the tears had stopped now, and he was enduring the biggest headache he'd ever had in his life. His forehead was now crusted over with drying blood and some of his hair stuck to it as he tried to wipe it free.

Eventually, Grady emerged from the shop again and locked the door behind him.

"You had a key?" Ethan raised an eyebrow, "This whole time?"

"First night I've ever used it," Grady admitted. "I was never sure why she gave it to me. I guess she hoped I'd return to her one day. Surely, not like this."

"I'm sorry." Ethan wasn't sympathetic to the destructive witch but he couldn't imagine what it would be like to see someone you had once cared for decapitated right before your very eyes. Sadly, he knew Grady had seen such horrors on more than one occasion.

"Thank you." Grady sat down on the steps next to Ethan. He ran his hands through his hair and rubbed his temples momentarily before finally taking a deep breath of his own. Ethan had come to translate this order of motion as a visual cue Grady was resetting himself.

"This is all my fault." Grady shook his head. He cast his gaze to the moon as well. Ethan regaled it as the one piece of the night that knew all of their secrets.

"No, it's not. This would've happened even if I'd never met you. It's *because* I met you that I'm still alive."

"What are you talking about?" Grady scoffed. "You were the one who defeated Marius."

"Not without the help of friends. *We* defeated Marius. I couldn't have done it without you or Dacey. I'm still too new to all of this. I still felt scared. But you guys, you guys were the brave ones."

"No, Ethan," Grady corrected, appraising him kindly. "Bravery is when you do the right thing even when you're terrified."

"He sacrificed himself for us," Ethan said. Sadness gripped his words and caused his throat to tighten.

"For you."

"You're wrong." Ethan looked at Grady with conviction. "He did it for us. Not just me. He saw us as a team. He knew what we could be capable of. He wanted us both to survive so we could face the world together."

"Do you really believe that?" Grady's words were wrapped with bittersweet happiness.

"With all of my heart," Ethan answered. "Dacey knew better than the both of us all along."

"I think you're right about that," Grady agreed with a warm smile.

"Let's go home," Ethan decided.

Happily surprised, Grady asked, "Do you still consider it that?"

"Why, are you kicking me out?" Ethan teased. He would definitely be taking every opportunity he got to harass the man. He deserved at least that much retaliation.

"Of course not," Grady laughed and looked at Ethan wistfully.

"What's that look?" Ethan wondered, smiling.

"It's the look of a man who thought he had nothing left to live for only to realize everything was right before him all along."

"Are you having life regrets, Doctor?" Ethan teased again.

"Greatly so," Grady sighed.

"Don't. Without your past...without your mistakes, we may have never met," Ethan said seriously. "I might not even be alive right now. I found out tonight, in the Dream World, my father had his own plans and Marius had been a part of that. I'll tell you about that all later, but the point I'm trying to make is I think we were supposed to meet. I know you don't believe in God or destiny or whatever you want to call it, but...I mean, what are the odds of you stumbling across Arthur's book halfway across the world? Sure, you went about the recruitment all wrong but I think we were supposed to end up together. We're meant to be a team. Together...we have the potential to save so many lives. To save the world. Worlds even."

"Slow down," Grady laughed. "You're the one with the power to do all of that. I have nothing special to offer."

"Sure you do," Ethan said.

"And what's that?" Grady wondered.

"You give me strength," Ethan answered.

ON THE DRIVE home, Ethan told Grady all about Kit and the things he'd learned from her in the Dream World. They decided together they would do more research into trying to discover the truth about how his father, Vincent Roam, had died. Grady also seemed open to Ethan's idea of capturing creatures and transporting them out of the world rather than killing them. For the first time, Grady was the one listening to Ethan's advice.

Ethan realized the scales had tipped in their relationship. He was no longer Grady's apprentice. Grady now viewed him as the one in control. He had become the voice of hope and reason. He was the new leader of their duo. Of course, Ethan didn't view it quite that way. He saw them more as equals. But if Grady felt he needed him to guide him then that's what he would do. He believed that's what they were meant to do. To make each other better.

The party seemed to have long disbanded and it was silent as they entered the huge house. Not even Benny had come to greet them. On the ride over, Ethan had wondered if with Marguerite gone that meant Benny's curse had been lifted? Grady had advised curses were much more powerful than spells and so, while eventually it would subside, it could take an indefinite amount of time to wear off.

They headed upstairs to call it a night, both moving toward their respective bedroom doors.

"One more thing," Ethan said, as Grady had opened his door to disappear inside. "Grady Hunter. That isn't your real name. Do you trust me with the truth?"

"I trust you with my life.".

"I promise I'll never repeat it," Ethan smiled, coaxing him.

"Alexander Quinn," Grady finally revealed. "I'm a wanted serial killer back home. There were several deaths during that time caused by Marius. Of course, because I was found in connection with Ava's it became the popular belief I was the cause of all of them. Can you imagine? Me? A serial killer? Ridiculous. Unless you count supernaturals, I suppose. I have killed quite a number of them."

"You make yourself sound like a real catch," Ethan joked, leaning against his own closed door.

"I don't have to be. I'm the one that caught you, remember?"

"Are you sure about that?" Ethan bit his lower lip. His bold gaze caused Grady to finally be the one with a blush across his cheeks.

"Would you..." Grady cleared his throat in an uncharacteristically nervous manner. "Would you like to stay with me tonight?"

He opened his door the rest of the way as he extended the invitation. Ethan's heart leapt. This time he wasn't embarrassed or shy as he made his way over to the man he loved. That timid person he used to be was left to the past. He was bold now. He was brave. He knew what he was. Who he was. Who he loved. What he lived for. Ethan kissed Grady with wild desire. His fearlessness gave permission to Grady's longing and his hands navigated Ethan's body, pulling off his sweater and tossing it to the ground. He caressed Ethan's neck with the trace of his soft lips. Ethan grabbed Grady by his collar and ushered him into the room. With the flick of his wrist, he used his powers to close and lock the door behind them.

Through the rest of the early morning hours, they explored a new world together that was entirely of their own design.

WHEN GRADY WOKE late in the morning, he rolled over to embrace Ethan but he was no longer there. He quickly sat up and threw back the sheets in fear something horrible had happened. Pulling on his clothes, he ran out of his bedroom only to see the door to Ethan's room was open and the light was on.

Grady regained his calm and strolled into find the young man, already dressed for the day, lying on his bed and holding on to the dream catcher. He'd obviously showered and cleaned up his wounds from the previous night's battle as well. He also had the copy of *The Mechanics of Sleep Travel* Arthur had gifted him sitting beside him. He'd obviously been very busy for quite some time.

"How stupid of me," Grady said. "Of course you wouldn't have been able to sleep in my room."

"It's all right." Ethan smiled at him. "The fun part had nothing to do with sleeping."

Grady grinned.

"Anyway, I was thinking about getting rid of this," Ethan said, tossing him the dream catcher. Grady caught it effortlessly.

He raised a brow. "Oh?"

"Yeah," Ethan said. "My dad seemed to manage fine without one. I have to learn how to function. I can't be scared of myself anymore."

Grady set the dream catcher down on Ethan's dresser and joined him by sitting on the edge of his bed.

"Just don't become reckless," Grady advised.

Ethan laughed.

"Yeah, because you know I'm such a rebel." Then, in seriousness, he grabbed Grady's hand affectionately and said, "I want to go."

"What?" Grady asked with alarm.

"I want to travel," Ethan said excitedly, sitting up. "I want to see everything. Go everywhere. I want to roam like I was meant to do. You were right. It's instinctual for me. It's who I am and I …I can't stop thinking about it."

"I finally have you and now you want to leave me." Grady couldn't suppress his disappointment.

"Not forever. Just…for a little bit," Ethan said softly. "I want to know what's out there."

"Obviously, I can't stop you," Grady said. "But…I won't pretend I don't hate the idea."

"I know," Ethan said. He leaned forward and kissed Grady gently. "I'll be safe, though. I'll be right here and you can watch over me. Check in on me. And if you ever think something might be wrong then you can summon me. Just…don't do it too soon, okay?"

"How long will you be gone?" Grady asked. His voice was tired.

"I don't know," Ethan answered honestly. "But I'll try not to be too long. You know I'll miss you like crazy."

"Not as much as I will you," Grady said. "You'll be distracted with the beauty of the infinite universe. All I'll have here to keep me company are my books and my paintings."

"And Benny," Ethan pointed out.

"Not comparable in the least," Grady said pointedly. Ethan laughed.

"I still want us to do everything we said we would last night," Ethan assured him. "But I want to be properly prepared for it. I need the experience."

"I understand. I don't like it but I understand," Grady conceded.

"Thanks." Ethan smiled.

"Oh! I did practice some after you fell asleep last night," he added, adorably excited to show off his newly honed skills. "Watch this!"

Almost effortlessly he produced a glowing white orb of energy and threw it across the room. It propelled itself with a higher velocity than he'd expected and hit an antique armchair in the corner of the room with extreme prejudice. The chair practically exploded, shattering into a thousand pieces.

Grady stared at him with shock. "That chair was over two hundred years old!"

Ethan cringed. "Sorry. Still learning."

Grady chuckled. Even after everything they'd been through, and how much he'd grown, Ethan was inherently still the same sweet and innocent man he'd fallen for.

"I guess you're right. You do need more experience." Grady winked at him. "When are you going?"

"I thought now would be good."

"Now?" Grady was surprised. "You don't even want to have breakfast first? Or, a second round of last night's escapades?"

"The latter is very tempting," Ethan said with a grin, lying down on the bed. "But then I might lose my resolve to actually go."

"Not seeing a problem with that."

"Yes, it has to be now," Ethan insisted. "I'll be back before you know it."

Grady sighed in compliance.

"What about you?" Ethan asked. "What will you do while I'm gone?"

"Well, I've spent the past two decades trying to avenge someone who I loved. Now, I believe it's time to put all of my efforts into protecting someone who I love."

It must have been the right answer because Ethan grinned like he was the luckiest person in existence.

"I'll be here by your side, probably doing a lot of research on that unresolved vampire problem and hoping for your speedy and safe return," Grady finished.

Ethan took Grady's hand again and held it to his heart. "No matter where I go or what I see out there, this world will always be my favorite because you're in it."

Grady smiled and leaned forward to kiss Ethan tenderly on the forehead.

"Sweet dreams, traveler," he whispered.

Grady watched lovingly as Ethan finally let himself relax, took a deep breath, closed his eyes, and transported himself across worlds.

About the Author

Dez Schwartz writes Dreampunk, Paranormal Fiction, and Gaslamp Fantasy about dream travelers, vampires, and dapper occultists. Her stories mostly feature LGBTQ leads. She resides in a haunted Edwardian era Texas home with her family and pirate crew of pets.

Email: dezschwartzauthor@gmail.com

Facebook: www.facebook.com/DezSchwartz

Twitter: @dez_schwartz

Instagram: @dezschwartzauthor

Website: www.dezschwartz.com

Also Available from NineStar Press

Connect with NineStar Press

Website: NineStarPress.com

Facebook: NineStarPress

Facebook Reader Group: NineStarNiche

Twitter: @ninestarpress

Tumblr: NineStarPress